LADY, THIS IS MURDER

LADY, THIS IS MURDER

Peter Chambers

Chivers Press • G.K. Hall & Co.
Bath, England Thorndike, Maine USA

This Large Print edition is published by Chivers Press, England, and by G.K. Hall & Co., USA.

Published in 2000 in the U.K. by arrangement with the author.

Published in 2000 in the U.S. by arrangement with Peter Chambers.

U.K. Hardcover   ISBN 0-7540-4295-2   (Chivers Large Print)
U.K. Softcover   ISBN 0-7540-4296-0   (Camden Large Print)
U.S. Softcover   ISBN 0-7838-9257-8   (Nightingale Series Edition)

The text of this Large Print edition is unabridged.
Other aspects of the book may vary from the original edition.

Set in 16 pt. New Times Roman.

Printed in Great Britain on acid-free paper.

British Library Cataloguing in Publication Data available

Library of Congress Cataloging-in-Publication Data

Chambers, Peter, 1924–
    Lady, this is murder / by Peter Chambers.
        p. cm.
    ISBN 0-7838-9257-8 (lg. print : sc : alk. paper)
    1. Private investigators—Fiction. 2. Large type books. I. Title.
    PR6066.H463 L34 2000
    823'.914—dc21   00–059677

CHAPTER ONE

A thin shaft of watery sunshine suddenly filtered through the smog outside the window and picked up a speck of dust on the otherwise immaculate surface of my desk. I stared at it with irritation. For twenty minutes I'd been sitting there, devoting my entire attention to that polished top, and now there was a flaw. The buzzer on the inter-com jagged harshly and I turned my gaze away from the speck long enough to flick down the key.

'Yup.'

'There's a Mr. Benson called to see you, Mr. Preston.'

Florence Digby's coolly impersonal voice came through the mesh.

'Well, I'm pretty busy, Miss Digby. Make an appointment, will you?'

It was four in the afternoon. Whatever I might be needing from the rest of this day, it did not include anybody named Benson. Before I could push the key to the up position Florence was back.

'Mr. Benson is from San Francisco, Mr. Preston. He has to return there tonight.'

Trying to keep the resignation from my voice I replied:

'Very well. Ask him to come in, please.'

A few seconds later Florence opened the

door, and I got a look at my visitor. He was sixtyish, with a strong, craggy face and hard black eyes. Unruly white hair sprang defiantly from the rather large head. He was medium height, but broad in the shoulder. If the dark grey suit had cost less than three hundred dollars, he'd cheated the tailor.

'Mr. Preston.'

'How are you, Mr. Benson?'

I stood up and we swapped a brief handshake. His palm was cool and dry, the grip strong. The black eyes raked me over, then did a quick appraisal of the layout. He parked in the visitor's chair, refused a cigarette. His bearing was authoritative but not pushy. At the back of my mind was something telling me I'd seen this man before, but it hadn't registered yet. So far all he'd said was my name, so I was mildly surprised to detect an unmistakable accent when he next spoke. An accent that started out in life less than a thousand miles from the Bay of Naples.

'Can that lady out there hear us talking?'

'No. The door is three inches thick,' I replied.

'O.K.' He turned the black eyes on me again. 'They tell me you're pretty smart feller.'

'They do? Who would they be?'

He shrugged.

'You know. People. Here, there. Around. I hear about you.'

Carefully I said:

2

'Then they probably told you I'm kind of an expensive feller too.'

He grinned briefly. At the side of his mouth a gold capping appeared and was gone as his lips closed.

'I always want the best. You want the best, you gotta pay for it. It figures.'

Almost without his being conscious of it, his left hand stroked at the beautiful lapel of his jacket. It seemed to me he'd got past the days when he rushed out to tell everybody how much he paid for everything, but still retained a lingering awareness of those times.

'Sure, they tell me about you. Also, I think about you before I come. Way I see it, a guy is smart, a guy makes a lot of money, that guy knows how to keep his mouth shut. Especially a guy in your business.'

This had all the markings of an offer to involve me in something the law wouldn't like.

'Mr. Benson,' I said slowly, 'you haven't told me why you're here, so no harm has been done. Yet. So before you go on, let me say something. I do know how to keep my mouth shut. But I don't get mixed up in things where I have to keep quiet or wind up in jail. So if there's anything a little bit—er—illegal about your business with me, we'll just say goodbye now, and no hard feelings.'

The grin was wider this time, and it wasn't one gold capping, it was two.

'Careful, too. But you don't hafta worry.

This is on the up-and-up strictly legit, I promise you. But it is confidential.'

'All right. Suppose you tell me about it,' I suggested.

He nodded, pushed thick spatulate fingers through the bristling white thatch on his head.

'Let's start with names,' he said. 'You been sitting there trying to place me. I'll put you out of your misery. The name is not Benson. It's Benito. I'm Rudy Benito.'

And of course that was why I remembered him. It had been some time now since his face was almost a daily feature in the rags. His hair had been black too, which helped to throw me. Rudy Benito. He'd been accused of practically every crime in the calendar at one time or another. In the early days, while he'd been learning his trade, the law actually caught up with him a few times. Then, as he moved up in the world, he became part of the élite of the crime ranks. The country club thug, the business man with as many legitimate enterprises as the other kind. Around the Bay, you didn't even knock over a filling station unless you got clearance from Benito. Not unless you had a fancy for late-night handicap swimming, the handicap being a barrel of cement on your feet. Florence Digby had been kidding when she told me our visitor was from San Francisco. Benito was San Francisco.

'The name is familiar, Mr. Benito,' I told him.

4

'I imagine,' he returned drily. 'So what do I want with you? That's what you're asking yourself, huh?'

I inclined my head.

'The thought had crossed my mind. On the one hand, unless my information is very much out of date, you already have a great number of—business contacts. People who could do anything I can do, probably quicker. They would have better sources of information, for instance.'

'Correct,' he agreed. 'And on the other hand?'

'On the other hand, you don't make a habit of wasting your time. So maybe there is something I can do for you. And when you're ready, you'll get around to telling me.'

'O.K.'

He suddenly snapped his fingers together. I didn't know then it was just a habit.

'O.K., Preston, now I tell you the story. The confidential story. I used to be married one time, you ever hear about it?'

'No, I didn't know.'

'Good. Not many people know. I don't rent television space to advertise it, if you get what I mean.'

I got what he meant.

'It was years ago, and it didn't take. I was pretty wild them days, you know, stick-ups, shootings. Rough stuff. It was before I got smart. If I'da had the good sense in my head to

5

hitch up with the kind of dames I was used to, it woulda done no harm. But I hadda go and pick a real straight girl, you know, from a good home and all. So naturally, she give me the air. Oh, she stuck it a while, coupla years maybe, but it wasn't no life for a woman like that. Guess I wasn't much for a woman like that either, or any other kind of woman. So she took the air one fine day.'

He spoke in a matter-of-fact voice, carefully watching the words so that he gave no hint as to how he felt about it all. He succeeded too. I couldn't have guessed whether his broken marriage had affected him or not. It was simply a recital of facts.

'After that I only saw her three or four times. She died about two years later. Pneumonia.'

Now a shadow flitted quickly across the heavy features. He smiled quickly, erasing the shadow immediately. But it had been there.

'Man, this is all hearts and flowers, huh? Well anyway, there isn't a lot more. We had a kid. A baby girl. We called her Gina, after her mother. Fine, nice kid. Beautiful. Naturally, the kid went with her momma. No place for a baby to be, bummin' around with guys like me. After her mother died, I kind of took the kid over, you know? Didn't keep her around me, natch. I put her in a swell convent up-state. They took care of her fine, brought her up a real fine person. l used to get up there when I

6

could, you know, like take her out to see the sights. All that. Then before you know it, she's eighteen and she has to quit school. I don't need to tell you the next bit.'

He looked to me for an answer.

'Just as a guess,' I hazarded. 'She probably came to San Francisco and it wasn't long before she found out something about your business interests. Something she didn't like.'

'Right. I didn't want it that way. I wanted to get her to move away, maybe New York or some place. But she wasn't going to have it. Said she'd been away from home long enough. Anyway that's the story. She told me she couldn't take that kind of life. Or me either, if that was the way I wanted to live. Yessir, I'm telling you the nuns did a great job on that girl. Sounds kinda crazy but I was real proud of her, way she told me off there.'

'When was all this?' I queried.

He screwed up his face and concentrated.

'This would be three—no—four, four and a half years ago.'

'So she's rising twenty-three now,' I commented.

Again the shadow. This time there was no grin to wipe it away.

'Let me tell you the story,' he went on. 'Well, my Gina walked out on me, just like momma. She came down-state, down to Vale City. Took an apartment, got herself a job. She wouldn't take any money from me, no help of any kind. I didn't push it too hard, either. Way she was feeling, she might just decide to go off again and maybe this time I don't find her so easy. At least this way I can get the word on her now and then, know how she's making out. If I should let her go wander off by herself, who knows what can happen. Young dames on their own in big towns, I've seen 'em. I know what happens. Oh, I forgot to tell you she changed her name, too. No more Gina Benito. Now suddenly, she's Jeannie Benson, and nobody down here puts a line from her to me. Anyway, I know she's O.K., that's what counts, so I let it ride.'

He was talking more slowly now, and I knew we were getting to the hard part.

''Bout a year ago she takes up with a guy over there in Vale. Little old for her, close to forty years old, but a legitimate guy. Councilman, too. I kept out of it. This might be a big thing for Gina, and she sure didn't want me lousing it up. So I kept away, huh? Looked like they might get married, even. Then suddenly, she ups and runs. Quits her job, the apartment, everything. Just left Vale one night and disappeared. Nobody knew where. I put some people on to it, but they couldn't turn anything up. That was six months ago. For half a year I haven't known where she is. I know now.'

Reaching inside his pocket he pulled out a tear-sheet from a newspaper. I looked at it and

8

saw it was from the previous day's edition of the L.A. *County Examiner.*

'Read it.'

There was a picture of a dyed blonde with an old-young face. The face had the glassy stillness of death. I'd read the story casually the day before, now I took in every detail. The headline said:

DOPE-GIRL FOUND DEAD

'Ruby Capone, aged about twenty-seven, was found dead in her apartment early this morning, apparently from an over-injection of heroin.

'Her fully-clad body was found by a friend, Miss Rose Schwartz, who lived in the next apartment at the Villa Marina. The police have issued a statement that the possibility of murder cannot be ruled out at this stage.

'The girl was a well-known figure in the clubs and bars of Monkton City and was arrested last month with three other girls from the Peek-a-Boo Club on charges alleging immorality. The charges were dropped, and Miss Capone was reported to be entering an action against the city for wrongful arrest.'

That was all there was. I read it again, memorising all the details. Then I handed it back to Benito.

'This is your daughter?'

9

He nodded, turning his head quickly away, but not before I caught a sudden added brightness in his eyes. When he spoke his voice was flat and controlled.

'That's Gina. I just found out about it by chance. Don't read that sheet as a rule. I bought it to pass the time while I was getting a blow-out fixed yesterday. That's how a man finds out about what happened to his own daughter. He reads about it in the paper in some lousy garage. I might never have known.'

He paused, but it wasn't the kind of pause where he was waiting for me to say something. We sat there in silence for a few moments.

'I want you to find out about this, Preston. You find out what was done to my Gina, and who did it. More than that. You find out what she's been doing these six lousy months, and who with. You don't worry about money. Spend what you need. More. Is it a deal?'

I thought about it. Thought a lot of things, mostly about why a man like Benito, a big underworld name, should come to me for this kind of work. Benito would have connections with tendrils which would reach deep down into the rotten core of Monkton or any other town. A solo operator like me, by comparison with the set-up he could command, would look like an elephant stamping on eggs.

'Why not just wait and see what the police can dig up?' I asked him.

He made a face.

'The cops? You trying to kid me, Preston? Whaddya think the cops gonna do? They gonna put to work extra help over this? Don't get me wrong. I don't think they're dumb. You don't find anybody get to where I got to in my business if he thinks the law boys are dumb. But what do they got? A cheap tramp dies from the big H. Whadda they suppose to do? She got no family, she got a phoney name. Nobody knows nothing about her, or if they do know a little something they don't gonna spill it to no cops. So they poke around a little, maybe they even try. But they're up a dead end, and they know it before they start. A tramp like this Ruby Capone, they say, whaddya want? It happens every day. After two, three days they know they're licked. Smart people, the cops. You don't find them banging their heads against no wall. They lose the file.'

I found myself nodding in involuntary agreement. What Benito said was true. The cities were full of young girls who came from nowhere and seemed to be heading for the same place. There was nothing wrong with the intentions of the police. It was just that they learned quickly how to recognise the signs when they came up against one more death like that of Ruby Capone.

Although Benito's voice was still under control, his vocabulary was slipping back to its natural expression as he talked on, a sure sign

11

of emotional disturbance.

'Have you thought about going to them yourself?' I questioned.

'You were her father, you can tell them everything about her up to a few months ago. With that kind of information they could—'

'Nah,' he grimaced. 'That's out. People like me we don't go to the law. For one thing it ain't natural, and another, there's people around might not feel too good about me getting cozy with a bunch of flatfeet. Wouldn't look right, wouldn't be right. We need something done, we got our sources. Anyway,' he looked at me bleakly, 'there's another reason. This Ruby Capone, she's nothing to me. I had a sweet girl, her name was Gina Benito, or even Jeannie Benson if she liked that better. She had no part of bars, dope and stinking things like that. She lived like what she was, a sweet clean girl, and that's the way she died. Jeannie Benson had friends, nice people. She had those nuns up there at the convent. You don't imagine I'm gonna have people like that getting my Jeannie mixed up with this Ruby Capone, huh?'

I knew what he was trying to say.

'No, I guess not,' I agreed.

'You guess good,' he told me.

'Well, if we're only concerned with Ruby Capone,' I suggested, 'what about those sources you were just talking about? They could tell you all you want to know. And in

12

about a quarter of the time it would take me to find out. Supposing I can, that is.'

He shook his head.

'Sure, I got sources. I could pick up that telephone right now,' he pointed at the desk, 'right now I could talk to a man. He'd have me the whole story inside of an hour. But I can't do that. Something is gonna happen to the guys who did what they did to Ruby Capone. And the organisation wouldn't understand. We don't have no personal fights in the organisation. They'd fix me sure.'

This didn't sound in character with what I knew about the man facing me. People had called him most things one time or another, but the word coward was never mentioned.

'Would that matter? I mean, even supposing you were right, and they did get to you, would it matter if you'd already nailed the people you want?'

Again the thick white hair wagged sideways.

'It wouldn't matter. Nothing matters any more. I'm not getting through to you, Preston. I know the organisation, know it from front to back. If something has to be done it gets done fast. For me, that could be too fast. They might get to me before I'm finished what I gotta do. And that, that, Preston, would matter.'

This man was really on his own, I reflected. There were two large, well-organised machines, either one of which could run down the people he wanted, the police department

13

and the mob. Both were denied to him. That seemed to leave only somebody like me.

'Well, Preston, whaddya say?'

Again the voice was unemotional, but I knew he cared about the answer.

'Tell me one thing,' I hedged. 'Let's suppose I buy. Let's suppose I get lucky, maybe find out what you want to know. Or, more accurately, who you want to know about. Then what happens? Are you going to blast whoever it is?'

The black eyes narrowed as he looked into my face.

'The way you say that, it don't sound like you'd care one way or the other.'

I ignored that.

'You haven't answered me,' I pointed out.

'All right, I'll answer you.' He kneaded the thick hands together. 'I'd like to, I'd like nothing better. I'd do it slow and I'd do it painful. And I'm telling you, Preston, I'd live every minute of it. If they'd killed this Ruby Capone I wouldn'ta given it a second look. But they did more. They killed somebody else, too. They killed my Jeannie. You might think that's all the more reason for me to take care of 'em personal. But killing Jeannie puts them out of my league. Guys like me don't have any connection with people like Jeannie Benson. You think I'm cockeyed, and I don't give a damn what you think. But the guys who did this, they're gonna be taken by the law. The

14

District Attorney is gonna get the whole works on everything these guys ever did, right down to spitting on the sidewalk. He is going to get an airtight, watertight, open and shut case on every count we can dig up. So tight that even Marty—even a big-league shyster won't get 'em off. And you are going to do the D.A. this big favour. Get it?'

'I think so,' I said slowly.

There were two things fighting inside this man. Every natural instinct in his thug make-up told him to go out and even the score for Jeannie. But this fixation he had about protecting her good name, trying to do things the way she would approve of, that was the thing keeping his hand off the trigger. And I hadn't overlooked the fact that he'd almost named the mob lawyer in his excitement.

'You appreciate I don't guarantee results?' I asked him.

'That means you'll give it a whirl, huh?'

'If you remember what I just said.'

Reaching inside his coat he pulled out a large manila envelope and laid it on the table in front of me.

'Expenses.'

I opened it. Inside were five large banknotes, and each one was valued at one thousand dollars.

'This buys my time,' I told him. 'It buys every effort I can make, all the bribes I have to put out. But it doesn't buy results, not

15

necessarily. Those I don't guarantee.'

I slid open a drawer by my hand and dropped the money inside. Benito nodded as if satisfied.

'You'll get results,' he stated. Then, 'All right, don't tell me again, I heard you the first time. But I think you'll do it.'

I said nothing to that. Instead I asked a question.

'This guy over in Vale City your daughter was friendly with. One you said was a councilman. You know his name?'

His face darkened.

'Now wait a minute, you're not interested in Jeannie Benson. Ruby Capone, that's your girl.'

'Agreed. But Ruby was born when Jeannie dropped out of sight. I'll have a better chance with Ruby if I can find out what Jeannie was doing just before she quit Vale.'

He brooded on it for a moment. Then:

'Well O.K., yeah, I guess so. You know your business better than me. Just so you have it straight. Nobody but you and me knows what happened to Jeannie. It better stay that way. The guy's name is Handford. Walter F. Handford. Runs a construction business out there. You watch your step in Vale City, Preston.'

'I'll watch it,' I told him. 'By the way, do you have a picture of Jeannie?'

'I do,' he confirmed. 'But I'm not gonna give

16

it to you. She looked nothing like that tramp Capone, tell you that much. You get the morgue picture of Ruby Capone. Nobody will ever know she's my Jeannie. You're gonna see it stays that way.'

'O.K.,' I shrugged.

He got up.

'I'm going back to San Francisco tonight,' he told me.

'How will I hear from you?'

'I'll telephone,' I told him.

He told me three numbers where I could contact him at different times of the day. Suddenly he grinned.

'Funny thing, Preston, they told me you wouldn't work for me.'

'They did?'

'Sure. They said you were a tricky guy sometimes, but you wouldn't get mixed up with anybody like—well anybody in my line of business. They were wrong, huh? I guess five grand is a loud line in conversation.'

I shook my head.

'They weren't wrong, Benito. They told you right. I wouldn't do a thing for you.'

He flushed an angry red.

'What the hell is that supposed to mean?'

'I'm doing it for a nice girl named Jeannie Benson. She seems to have had the wrong breaks all through. So I'm going to do something for her now, if I can. And she wouldn't have had anything to do with you, either.'

A puzzled look came on his swarthy face, and he shook his head in bewilderment.

'They also told me you had a lot of funny ideas sometimes. Well,' he shrugged, 'I don't give a damn what your reasons are. You're doing it, that's what counts.'

It was a long time since anybody talked to Benito the way I was talking. If things had been different, so would his reactions. But things weren't different. We stared each other out for a while, then he went to the door.

'You noticed about the name, I guess? Ruby was as near as she could get to Rudy. She wasn't going to use the name Benito in case anybody tied me in. So what did she do? She had to pick a name that stinks everywhere. So I'd get the message if I ever found her. How much can you hate anybody?'

I hadn't any answer for that. Finally he shrugged and opened the door to leave.

'You'll call me, huh?'

'I'll call you.'

CHAPTER TWO

I parked outside the Villa Marina and made sure I didn't leave anything of any value in the Chev. The Villa Marina was a picturesque name for a picturesque place. The name had a

18

savour of old Spain, of rose-twined balconies and imperious fan-waving beauties. Picturesque. The building was an eight-storey flat-fronted apartment house, in the last stages of decay. The once-white walls were now a browny-grey, and it was anybody's guess what colour the paintwork had once been. Here, in the Harbour district, the smog was now fog, and this lingered clammily around me as I stood inspecting the outside of the last home of Ruby Capone.

It was almost seven in the evening, and night was steadily pushing the daylight over the horizon. There were lights in a number of windows, many of which didn't boast any curtains. The number of the apartment I wanted was seven. I stood in the entrance a moment, inspecting the name cards that were stuck at all angles in the slots opposite the apartment numbers. I noticed the blank at number five, as I pushed at the buzzer marked 'seven'. There was a click as the front door lock was disengaged. I pushed it open and went inside. It didn't take my nose long to decide the smell of the fog was preferable to the odours in the chipped and faded hallway.

The rankness of a hundred lifetimes of failure hung in the air. No place to linger I decided, making for the stairs.

Number seven was on the second floor, and I located the door, pressed the bell-push several times before it dawned on me the thing

19

was dead. Then I rapped loudly with my knuckles. After a short while the door opened. I was looking at a girl about twenty years old. No, not a girl. This had never been a girl, this was a fully matured, middle-aged woman. About twenty years old. She wore a plunging yellow satin dress which ended just above the knees. The edge of a grubby bra-strap leered out from one shoulder. Her hair was brass, coiled and twisted in astonishing shapes, and with the dull lifelessness of too much lacquer, too little soap. She had full, heavy breasts, and no inhibitions about who saw them, including me. The waist was still slender, but the hips and downwards were too meaty for a girl of her years. Her feet were encased in soiled pink mules.

'Miss Rose Schwartz?' I enquired politely.

'Was that you pushed my call-sign?'

Her voice was harsh, and matched the cunning suspicion in her heavy-lidded eyes.

'It was,' I confirmed. 'Like to have a little talk if you can spare a few minutes, Miss Schwartz?'

I dropped my voice confidentially, and she misinterpreted this completely. Immediately she lost the sloppy, careless attitude and pulled herself erect, the overweight mammalians sticking out at me aggressively. Raising one hand she preened at the back of her hair, and a mocking smile replaced the hard lines of her orange-painted mouth.

20

'You got your nerve, handsome, coming round here to my place like this. I gotta strict rule about that, I thought everybody knew. Still, now you're here and all, might as well come in for a minute. Mind you, any funny business and out you go.'

She stood to one side to let me in, but not so far that I could avoid rubbing against one of the huge projections on her bosom. She chuckled.

'Fresh, ain't you?'

I didn't want to say anything else till I was inside. Miss Rose Schwartz, retiring violet as she was, would be capable of screaming the place down at the slightest provocation. And talking of provocation, she'd closed the door carefully and was now leaning against it. Her hands were behind her back, and one leg was pressed against the other and slightly forward so that the whole curve of her thigh was thrust into relief against the sheer material of the tight-fitting dress. Miss Rose Schwartz had misread the purpose of my visit, and I only knew one thing that would pacify her when she found out her mistake.

'You got your nerve, big feller,' she repeated.

I nodded, pulled out my billfold, peeled off two tens and a five. Rose scowled, not too much.

'You don't have a helluva lot of finesse, do you?'

21

'Finesse is something I keep for when I'm playing cards,' I told her.

She grinned, in what she hoped was an alluring fashion. It came out like the knowing leer of a five-dollar whore.

'You shouldn't oughta waste your time with those old card games,' she said. 'I know some fine little games for a coupla nice people like you and me.'

Before she could pursue that any further I asked:

'Is there a drink around?'

This she understood.

'Sure,' she nodded. 'Tell you what, I like you. Got some cheap wine out there for people I don't like. Wait, I'll get you a man's drink.'

She disappeared through a door. I looked around the room for somewhere to sit. It was a jumble of cheap furniture, glossy magazines, overflowing ashtrays. There was dust everywhere, and anybody could see the delectable Rose was nobody's home girl. On balance, I thought I'd skip sitting down.

She came back carrying two tumblers, both dirty, one of them cracked. Each was half-filled with an amber liquid.

'Scotch,' she announced proudly. 'Well, skol.'

I sipped gingerly at the drink. It bit into my tongue like molten lead. If this was Scotch, the distiller must have dropped his claymore into

22

the vat. Rose emptied half her drink with every appearance of relish. She was either a very good actress or she had an asbestos throat. Setting the tumbler down she came close to me and moved to take the bills from my hand. I hung on to them and tutted.

'I read in a book once, never let anybody get their claws on the coin until you've handled the goods.'

She gave me the leer again.

'So handle the goods. Who's stopping you?'

Nobody was stopping me. In fact it was practically impossible for me to move a muscle without handling some part of the overflowing charms of this reticent maiden.

'Here.'

I thrust one of the tenspots into her hand. She looked at me in puzzlement. Not that it prevented her from latching on to the bill.

'You got a strange approach, lover.'

But she was still a long way from hostile— ten dollars worth away.

'Well, that's it,' I informed her. 'When I get close to a woman all I want to do is talk.'

'Talk?' she echoed, but she moved one pace away. 'Hey, you're not some weirdo, are you?'

I shook my head.

'Uh uh. I'm harmless. Just like to talk.'

'Who sent you here?'

Her voice was hardening with suspicion again.

'A man. You wouldn't know him. Sent me to

have a talk with you.'

She was scared now, backing away as she spoke. Scared because the door behind her was shut, and she knew she could never get it open before I reached her. When you live like Rose, you live on the edge of disaster. The disaster doesn't always have a face or a form. It's a nameless horror that lurks in the distance, beckoning. Rose was beginning to think this was her time for that encounter.

'A—a talk,' she whispered, trying to force confidence back into the words. 'Sure, we'll talk. I like to talk. What would you like to talk about, mister?'

'Don't be scared,' I tried to sound gentle, 'I'm not here to hurt you.'

'Yeah?'

She wanted to believe that. Wanted desperately to believe it, but who could believe a guy with no red blood in him. A guy who'd just rejected a golden opportunity? All these thoughts played across her face, plain to be read.

'Sit down, Rose. Here,' I held out my glass, 'have another drink. It's early for me anyway.'

She nodded, never taking her eyes off me as she came slowly forward. As though hypnotised she took the glass and tipped some of the drink into her mouth. Then, nodding as if to reassure me, she went and sat down facing me.

'Fine,' I said. 'Now look, you have this all

24

wrong. All I want to do is talk to you a few minutes. Then I'll leave you the rest of the money, and blow. You'll probably never see me again.'

She liked the last part, about the money and never seeing me again. Especially never seeing me again.

'All right, let's talk, why not?'

'Why not?' I agreed. 'Let's talk about Ruby.'

The returning confidence vanished again as though someone flipped a switch.

'Ruby?'

'Sure. Ruby Capone. Tell me about her.'

She shook her head, eyes wide.

'I don't know anything about her. Nothing. She was just Ruby. She lived next door. Yesterday she died, I found her. That's all there is. There's nothing to know.'

'I'm disappointed, Rose. I thought you liked to talk.'

'Listen,' she pleaded. 'I'm levelling with you. Sure, I like to talk. But what's to talk about? I told you all I know about Ruby.'

I looked at her with a pained face.

'That's what you told the police, Rose. That's fine. Nobody should talk to those guys about anything. But this is different, this is for me. And for twenty-five bucks.'

'Huh,' she snorted. 'You know where I can get a new face for twenty-five stinking dollars?'

'No, I don't. Who's going to damage the one you've got, if you tell me about Ruby?'

25

She bit her lip.

'I don't know anything about Ruby,' she insisted sullenly. 'Leave me alone.'

'I am leaving you alone,' I pointed out. 'Well, if you won't talk, O.K. Seems a pity, though. You're kind of hot right now, Rosie. Some little guys are worrying about you, worrying about what you know. They might decide to do something about you, and that would be a shame. You see, there's big guys interested in all this. Big guys what don't stand for any little guys thinking like they're big guys too. But you do it your way. It's your funeral.'

She was huddled in the chair, eyeing me watchfully.

'What big guys?' She was definitely interested. 'And quit talking about funerals.'

I decided to get free with Benito's five grand. I tossed the remaining fifteen dollars on to a table.

'Guys who use this kind of money for waiters,' I announced grandly.

It registered. Rose didn't see twenty-five dollars coming in her direction every day of the week. Especially for free.

'Keep it,' I told her. 'People I work for don't like me giving back bills that have been handled. Buy yourself something.'

She didn't believe it yet. There had to be a catch in there someplace. One thing I'll say for Rose, she should never play poker. Her emotions and thoughts marched across her face in a steady parade. I thought she was beginning to come round now. Suddenly, almost noiselessly, the door of the apartment swung open and a man stepped inside. He took in me, then Rose. A nasty small smile appeared on his weak face. He was in his early twenties, tall, thin and vicious looking. Straggly fair hair topped off the bony, skull-like face. When he spoke, his voice was an octave higher than a grown man's had any right to be.

'Who's he?' he demanded.

He was talking to Rose, but he kept looking steadily at me.

'Rose and I been having a little talk,' I advised him.

'That's a lie,' she shouted, and the fear in her voice was plain. 'He come bustin' in here, Took, threatened to push me around, but I didn't tell him a word. Honest, Took, not a word.'

Took pulled bloodless lips back from his grey teeth.

'It's all right, baby, I believe you. What did he want to talk about?'

'About Ruby. You remember poor Ruby, Took,' I said conversationally. 'She died in the next apartment yesterday.'

'You shut up,' he told me nastily. 'You, Rose, what'd you tell him?'

'Nothin', Took. Listen, I swear—' she said desperately.

'Not in front of me, lady, please,' I

entreated. 'Swearing is out.'

'I told you to button,' he reminded me. 'Otherwise you'll be out—out on the floor.'

'Tut, tut. Harsh words,' I remonstrated.

He ignored that, and addressed Rose from the side of his mouth.

'What about Ruby?' he demanded.

'Nothin',' she whined. 'Hell, I don't know. He didn't ask me nothin' that made any sense.'

'Take a look at the table,' I suggested. 'That make any sense?'

He took the dark green snakes eyes away for a fraction of a second, saw the money. When he looked back at me the eyes were narrower.

'What's the dough for, Rose?'

'That's not all,' I wanted to be as helpful as possible, 'Rose has another ten that she tucked away somewhere.'

The shivering girl now got up and went quickly to the thin one. Looking up into his face she pleaded with him.

'Look, you gotta believe me. I don't even know this guy's name. He crashed the joint, started raving about Ruby Capone. He put that money there sure, but not because I told him anything. Listen, you gotta believe that's the way it was. It's important.'

'I know it is, baby,' again the unpleasant grin. 'But maybe you've forgotten what's important. This slob comes in waving a few bills, and straight off you forget what's healthy

28

and what isn't, huh?'

'No, no,' she contradicted fiercely.

Running to the table she grabbed up the notes and pushed them at me.

'Here, take your filthy money and get outta here. You know I didn't do anything for it. Tell him, will ya?'

'Tell him what, Rosie?' I asked, in a mystified tone. 'I don't know what you want me to say.'

She looked at me in disbelief.

'No,' she muttered. 'You can't do this to me. Why would you wanta do this to me? I never done you no harm.'

There was no smile on Took's face now.

'I'll get to you in a minute, tramp.' Grasping the girl's arm he spun her out of the way. 'Now you, you better start talking.'

'Me?' I studied him carefully. 'I like talking to her. Don't think I'd enjoy talking to you. Don't like your face.'

I moved towards the door. He stepped quickly in front of it.

'Where d'ya think you're going?' he asked softly.

'Out,' I replied. 'You're in my way.'

He grinned as his right hand flashed away from his coat. There was a knife in it suddenly, four inches of narrow tapered steel that glittered unhealthily.

'Now then, what did you and Rose talk about?'

29

I watched his eyes all the time now he was holding the chiv. They were noticeably brighter and his breathing was slightly faster and he was breathing through an open mouth. These were recognisable signs and not encouraging. People carry knives for all kinds of reasons. Protection, intimidation, maybe just for kicks. Took wasn't in any of those categories. He had a knife because he enjoyed using it, had a need of it. I'd seen the pose before. With most people a knife is just a weapon, but with Took it was a part of him, as though you only got the complete Took when the knife was in his hand. As somebody once said, the weapon was an extension of the man.

I moved fast to the nearest chair, picked up an overstuffed cushion. His grin got wider, but he made no move to come after me. That was unnecessary. If I was going out, it had to be through the door, and as long as he stayed where he was that meant through him as well. I approached him carefully, and he bent very slightly at the knees. The knife was close to his body, point upwards. A position from which he could make short, jabbing thrusts without extending his arm. His eyes were glued to the cushion. I was three feet away now, and wishing it was three miles. A quick feint with the cushion brought a fast upward cutting movement that would have split my belly like a peapod if I hadn't immediately jumped back.

He laughed, a short breathless sound.

'Wanta talk now, buddy boy? Not too late yet.'

'I already told you, I don't like your face.'

Rose was pressed flat against the wall, horror and fascination battling for supremacy on her face. The shimmering steel seemed to hypnotise her as Took waved it gently from side to side.

A rivulet of cold perspiration ran down my cheek. Took noted it and nodded with satisfied pleasure.

'I'm going to slide this into your nice soft guts, buddy boy,' he whispered. 'Then I'm gonna pull it sideways like this,' he jerked the blade viciously to the right. 'Know what'll happen?'

I knew, but I didn't want to think about it. Instead I made another feint with the cushion, slightly wider this time. His reactions were fast and cool. Took wasn't going to let excitement cloud his judgment. As I moved in he brought the knife up once again in a fast stabbing movement, but returned it immediately to a waiting position once he found he hadn't made contact. Another man might have been excited enough to attempt a follow-up, another try. Not Took. Whatever thoughts I'd had about taking the knife in the cushion I'd have to forget. This man wasn't about to be caught like that. So I'd have to try something else, something that would leave me wide open if it didn't work. And I'd have to try it now,

31

because if I thought about it too long I'd talk myself out of it.

I went towards him for the third time, clutching the cushion convulsively as if it were a life-jacket. Took watched the cushion and my hands carefully, noting the mounting nervousness in my grip. I was trying, by every sign I could, to indicate that this was the time, and the cushion was my big hope. Now I was close enough. The cushion moved into him as before and he was ready for the inevitable attempt to get the knife wedged in the cushion and then a rush from me to throw him off balance. That was what I'd been trying to signal on my two abortive attempts, and that was what he was ready for. Instead I threw the cushion at his face. At the same moment I dropped my body backwards and as my feet came up off the floor I kicked hard at his groin. The knife was on its way upwards as I fell and my feet were coming up underneath it. He had no chance to reverse the blade before I made contact. I felt a primitive surge of pleasure as my shoe sank into softness and a deep sigh of agony hissed from the man by the door. The knife dropped from heedless hands as he grabbed instinctively for the pain. I hit the floor with a bruising thump and rolled immediately sideways. As I scrambled up Took was just bending forward to recover the blade. I was all footwork tonight. In two strides I was next to him, and my foot stamped hard on the clutching fingers. He screamed loud with rage and pain, and I chopped him across the back of the neck with the side of my hand. This time he was through. He fell forward in a crumpled untidy heap on the floor. Rose gasped.

'You killed him,' she said hoarsely.

'Not this time,' I contradicted, my voice shaky. 'You keep rough company, Rose. I imagine this guy will want to talk to you when he pulls round. Doubt whether you'll enjoy it.'

'Listen, mister, you can't leave me here with him.'

She pointed a trembling finger at the unconscious man.

'Why? You didn't tell me anything,' I reminded her. 'You don't know anything. Remember?'

I was sorry for Rose. Whatever she was mixed up in, I certainly wasn't helping her. But whatever it was, it had to be dirty, very dirty, for a guy like Took to be involved. It was just her bad luck that I wanted to know about Ruby Capone. Dames like Rose don't need a lot of sympathy wasted on them. In her own way she was just as vicious as Took.

'I'll be moving along,' I told her. 'Maybe I'll come and see you some other time. You might feel like telling me something, who knows?'

Slowly she shook her head, the fear still wide on her face.

'Not me, mister. Not now, not any time. I'm in bad enough trouble now, what you did to him. But I ain't said a word and I ain't going to. I don't know who you are, but you want some free advice you'll get out of this town. Just get, and keep travelling. You may get lucky, maybe they won't catch up with you.'

'Who won't?'

I asked the question from habit, but I knew there'd be no answer. Leaning down, I picked up Took's knife and stuck it in a pocket.

When I walked out of the door Rose was still in the same spot.

CHAPTER THREE

It's a funny thing about money. Everybody's always busy telling everybody else he doesn't get enough of it, yet the more he gets, the more he spends. Of course you have to take account of the social obligations. If a man were to hang on to his money, he'd very soon find he did have enough. So what would be left to talk about?

Around Monkton City, this desirable commodity is plentiful. In the early years of World War Two, the defence plant spillover from L.A. reached out as far as Monkton. For a while after that there was a period of transition to peace-time industries. Then the Korea thing put the area back on a wartime footing, and the town has never really looked back. The Industrial Association of Monkton City have a saying, 'You want it, we got it'. There isn't a single useless item of household equipment, not one pointless gadget you could name, that we don't produce around Monkton. That's where the smog comes from. Fifteen miles inland there are orange groves and sunshine, things people think of automatically when California is mentioned. Here, in this once sleepy harbour town, the sun ration is being reduced steadily but inexorably as the years pass. But like the man said, where's there's smog there's money. The population has quadrupled in twenty years, and the prime occupation of the people is getting rid of their money. They long ago got past the stage where they needed any reason to spend it. Now it's practically a compulsion. Once upon a time, if the people had a need for something, an obliging manufacturer produced it, and they bought it. Nowadays you just set up a plant and start producing something. It doesn't matter much what it is, you produce it and they'll buy it.

This change in the local spending habits has not gone unobserved by those who make a study of such matters. Those who regard it as their particular role to provide outlets for the spenders. Not all of these are manufacturers. There is another group of citizens closely interested in the destination of the spare dollars around the city. Their motives, alas, are not social. Not social at all. They are the denizens of an undesirable hunk of real estate called Conquest Street. Conquest starts out harmlessly enough at Fourth Avenue, which is the office section for the smaller businesses of the city. There is a legitimate theatre square on the corner of Conquest and Fourth, the Monkton City Opera House, no less. But, as I say, this is just at the beginning of the street. To reach the further end you have to traverse another eleven blocks, winding up at River Street. On the way you will be conscious of the changing nature of the entertainments on offer. The top end is a brilliantly lit thoroughfare with one or two passable restaurants, and a prestige movie house that specialises in foreign movies. The lower end, and the word is used advisedly, is hardly illuminated at all, and what some of the uninviting premises specialise in is something you don't want to dwell on.

The Peek-a-Boo Club is three-quarters of the way down, and although I'm not of a nervous disposition I removed my .38 Police Special from the glove compartment and slipped it under my arm before climbing out of the Chev. A sign over the door announced that the club was open to members only, but nobody mentioned it so I pushed open the door and went inside. It isn't much of a place, just a bar and a few booths with one end roped off to serve as a stage. Here, an upright piano

36

stood, but the lid was down and there was no sign of the fat character who usually insulted the keys.

I went to the bar and sat down. The bartender was a stranger to me, a burly man with a slight squint in his left eye. He leaned on the counter waiting for me to order something. I settled for a bottled lager. I don't usually drink it, but it was the only label on view I could identify as harmless. When he poured it I asked him:

'Took around?'

'Who?' he enquired suspiciously.

'Took. Tall thin guy. Nasty disposition. He's a pal of Ruby's.'

'I don't get it,' he told me. 'Ruby who?'

'Ruby Capone,' I said patiently. 'Wassa matter, you new here?'

He looked at me thoughtfully. While he did that, he was drawing his thumb along the line of his jaw. The thumb was about the size of a sausage and it rasped along the stubble like a buzz-saw.

'New?' he repeated. 'Well now, I been here a coupla months. But I been tending bar a lot longer. And I know when somebody is shooting off his mouth.'

I wagged my head sideways.

'You got it wrong,' I told him. 'Just want to talk to Took or else Ruby, if she's around.'

'Wait here a minute, I'll see if anybody ever heard of your friends.'

I watched him go through a door at the side. A moment later he stuck his head round the door and beckoned.

I went through into a narrow passage way, with doors leading off. The bartender pointed to the door opposite.

'In there,' he clipped.

'After you, brother,' I said politely.

Nobody in his right mind would turn his back on a man that size in a place like the Peek-a-Boo. He grinned, and the squint made his whole face evil.

'Nervous disposition, huh? Ya needn't worry. I'm heading back to the bar.'

'Fine,' I replied. 'I'll just watch.'

He hesitated, shrugged, then went back inside the club. I waited till he was behind his counter again. Then I crossed to the closed door, knocked and opened it. A man was sitting behind a small desk filing his nails. He had boot-polish hair and a small elegant moustache. He was wearing a dark grey well-cut suit and a heavy silk shirt and woollen tie. Also a lot of perfume. This guy thought very well of himself. After two more strokes with the file, to show who was waiting on who, he looked up casually.

'Who would you be?'

'I've often thought about it,' I returned. 'So many guys had a wonderful life. Maybe Churchill, maybe Errol Flynn. Lots of others, it's a tough question.'

He nodded.

'A clown. Why do I always get the clowns?'

'You'll be Vander, huh?' I hazarded.

'I'll be Mister Vander,' he corrected. 'You've heard of me, huh?'

'No,' I contradicted. 'I knew your brother Max, one time. He was an operator, that Max. Quite a guy. Rough, tough and a big hand with the dames. You look like Max might have looked if he lived on cream cakes for six months.'

A dark mottled flush bloomed suddenly on the fleshy face.

'Oh, yes,' he breathed. 'A real clown. What did you come here for, clown? A dentist would have got rid of your teeth without any pain.'

'Oh, pshaw,' I mocked. 'You're threatening me, Vander.'

The frown on his face was more puzzled than angry.

'I don't get it,' he commented. 'I never saw you before, but you come in here just begging to be kicked to death. Why?'

'Not by you, cream cakes,' I assured him. 'Max was different. Max was smart, and tough too. Maybe he could have taken me. We never did get around to finding out.'

'What's all this about Max? And what made him so smart? He didn't look so smart when the cops caught up with him in that warehouse. There were eight lumps of iron in Max when I identified the body.'

He pointed the nail file at me to emphasise what he was saying.

'Sure,' I agreed. 'But he lived high while he lived. You wouldn't have found him running a two-bit joint like this. And he wouldn't have been dumb enough to have anybody like Took on the payroll.'

'Ah.'

He wagged his head and the light of understanding came into his eyes.

'You're that one. You're the guy gave Took an argument tonight.'

I bowed.

'The same.'

'He was lucky, that's all.'

The door had opened softly, and framed in the opening was the man I'd left lying on the floor in Rose's apartment. He seemed overjoyed to see me.

'Got a friend of yours here, Took,' said Vander.

'I see him. How are you, buddy boy.' Took regarded me with unholy pleasure.

I ignored him. To Vander I said:

'Look, I'm getting a little sick of this guy, I tried to be nice to him a couple of hours ago. If he bothers me now I'll break his arm.'

Vander made no reply. Took closed the door as he came through.

'Which one will you break?'

He held them both out. In the right hand was another knife, first cousin to the one I'd

40

taken from him earlier.

'The one with the steel finger, naturally,' I told him. 'It wouldn't be any fun if I thought you could still come after me.'

He licked his lips, but not from nervousness. It was more the action of an animal viewing a meal. I felt differently about him this time. Differently because this time I was packing the difference under my left arm. If the going got really bad, I could always fall back on the gun. It did a lot for my confidence. Deliberately I turned so that I was sideways on to the knife expert, and spoke to Vander.

'One thing Max would never have done was hire a fairy.'

The club owner looked interested.

'A fairy?'

'Sure.'

I jerked a thumb towards Took, who didn't know quite what to do with a guy who pretended he wasn't there.

'Him. Rose and me, we were having a little fun, you know how it is. Then in busts Cutie Red Lips here and makes a big play for me. You know how these fags are. Well, I told him to scram.'

'You liar. You filthy liar,' Took hissed. 'You can't talk about me that way—'

Ignoring him I went on talking to the top man.

'He started to bawl, right in front of Rose. Well, I was disgusted—'

With a scream of rage Took flung himself at me, knife point extended. I turned towards him, dropping fast to one knee and turning inside the out-thrust arm, pushing it away with my right shoulder. The force of his rush almost knocked me forwards but I'd remembered to keep my left elbow pointed and rigid. It sank deep into his middle and he gave a mighty whoosh as all the air was expelled from him. Pushing upwards I rammed the back of my head into his face as I grabbed the arm with the knife. Despite everything else he still had a firm grip on the steel.

'Drop it, Took, or I'll break your arm,' I shouted.

By the way of reply he called me a name and at the same instant gave a mighty wrench to get the arm free. The wicked point came to within inches of my face before I could hold him. Quickly I brought up my right knee, relaxed the grip on his arm for a brief instant, then pushed down violently against the raised leg. There was a thin, snapping sound and a scream that died into a gurgle. The knife dropped from useless fingers and I let go of the arm. The forepart sagged, bringing a further howl of agony from Took. I stepped forward and clear of him, turning to look at his face. He was staring almost in disbelief at the dangling arm, quickly bringing his other hand to support it as another wave of pain hit him.

'You—you broke it,' he sobbed. 'You broke

my arm, you—'

He said things. I shrugged.

'This is the major-league. Rough company. No place for a guy who can only cut up dames.'

Vander sat where he was. Turning to him I said:

'You got any complaints?'

He looked at me expressively.

'The guy is a slob, just like you said. I been thinking of getting rid of him anyway. This about wipes him off.'

Leaning forward he touched a buzzer in the front of the table. Almost at once a large man loomed in the doorway.

'Took got into an argument, Ben,' Vander intoned. 'Take him to the sawbones. Get him patched up first class. The bill is on me. If we owe him any money, see he gets it. And give him an extra hundred besides. Kind of severance pay.' Turning to the ashen Took, he said softly, 'You heard all that. You got any little thing you wanta tell me?'

Dumbly, Took shook his head.

'When you're fixed up, clear town. I don't want you around, and I don't want anybody talking to you. There's people might not like it. Are you tuned in?'

'Sure, Mr. Vander, sure.' Took bit his lip. 'Say, give me a break, huh? You'll never hear of me again. Honest.'

Vander inclined his head.

'Sure, Took. Certainly. I'm convinced of it.

43

Now, you got no squawks with the way you've been treated. All the dough that's coming to you, and an extra century for carfare. Use it.'

His eyes narrowed slightly, and the voice was soft as the kiss of death.

'Tomorrow night I'll have one or two friends see if they can find you. You know, like for a little party.'

Took wagged his head up and down vigorously.

'You don't need to do that, Mr. Vander. Tomorrow night I'll be a thousand miles away.'

'Good. Ben.'

The big man nodded and Took walked slowly out, nursing the broken arm. He hadn't even looked in my direction since Vander started talking. The club owner sat back in his chair and had a look at me.

'You're a noisy kind of feller,' he observed. 'You always take on like this?'

'Only if somebody annoys me,' I replied. 'You're kind of hard on the help round here. Must turn over quite a staff.'

He jerked his head towards the door.

'That, you mean? That was nothing to do with you. That guy's been getting in my hair lately. Tonight about finished him. First off, bringing you here this way. Then pulling all that play in my own office. Guys are supposed to do what I tell them. I didn't tell him to go for you.'

'You didn't break a leg trying to stop him,' I

pointed out.

Vander heaved his expensive shoulders.

'Why should I? It was nothing to me. I don't know who you are, but you're some kind of trouble. Trouble I can always smell a mile off, and I can live without it. Without you, too.'

I took a pack of Old Favourites from my pocket, and lit one. Leaning confidentially on Vander's desk I blew a thin stream of smoke at him. His eyes glinted but he didn't say anything.

'I'm a friend of Ruby Capone's,' I told him.

For all the effect it had I could have been talking about the weather.

'Capone?' he repeated, making it a question. 'Would that be a relative of Al's?'

I grinned.

'Jokes, already. Last I heard from Ruby, she was working here for you. Now suddenly she's dead. I want to know a little something about the details.'

'Oh, that one,' he nodded. 'So many of these dames come in and out the place, I sometimes slip a name. What about her?'

'She's dead, that's what about her,' I reminded him. 'What do you want to tell me about that?'

He smiled, letting me admire the beautiful teeth.

'If you can read, you know as much as I do. It was all in the paper.'

I flicked ash on the table top. Vander noted

it, and put it down to my account.

'I read the paper. Seemed to me the Schwartz girl was calling on her old pal Ruby at a funny time of day. Three-thirty in the morning. Seemed to me somebody sent Rose there. Somebody like you.'

'You got a dull line in conversation,' he told me. 'Anyhow, I don't know anything about it, so beat it. I've got work to do here.'

'Cops have been wondering about this elegant place of yours for some time. Wondering whether it's really a junk-store. Think I'll go have a talk with them.'

I swung off the desk. Vander sat quite still for a moment. Then he said very quietly:

'You shouldn't have said that. You should have walked outa here nice and quiet. Now you spoiled it.'

'Really? What are you going to do about it?'

His hand moved quickly towards the buzzer. I brought the side of my palm down hard across the outstretched fingers. Vander cursed and began to get up. Pulling the .38 from inside my coat I held it between his eyes and clicked off the safety catch noisily. He froze, and the eyes glittered with fear.

'Why don't you sit down again?' I invited.

He sat, carefully. In his place I'd have done the same.

'We were talking about Ruby,' I suggested.

'Listen, she was just a dame worked here,' he insisted. 'You know how they are. They turn up from nowhere. A few weeks, maybe months it's like they live in the place. Then suddenly they go. You never see 'em again. That's how it was with Capone.'

'Uh huh.'

What he said was quite true. Dames like Ruby, and Rose Schwartz, they get a yen to move on, or maybe somebody takes them off on a trip, and when the trip's over they don't bother coming back. What Vander didn't know, at least what I was assuming he didn't know, was that Ruby Capone was making her first appearance in places like the Peek-a-Boo. Ruby hadn't yet become an aimless wanderer like the rest of the B-girls. And she never would now.

'When did you see her last?'

'I don't remember, exactly,' he sat there looking like a man trying to remember. 'Maybe a week, ten days. Who knows?'

'You know,' I told him. 'And you're a liar. Ruby was getting her supplies here. You're not telling me she suddenly got another source?'

'I don't know anything about that side of it,' he said doggedly. 'I got a steady place here with the booze and a few girls putting it out for me. What would I want with that kind of merchandise?'

'I wouldn't know,' I replied. 'And I don't care. Just tell me where Ruby got the stuff if it wasn't from you. Then I'll blow.'

He started to say he didn't know again, but I

suddenly pushed the black metal of the automatic close up to his face again.

'Listen, I don't know exactly. But there's somebody outside who could maybe tell me.'

'Yeah? Who?'

'One of the girls. Name of Lola. I don't know the rest of it. But she's on the stuff, and she was buddies with this Capone. Maybe she can tell you something.'

'O.K. Let's go ask her.'

I jerked the .38 and Vander got up watching me like a cat the whole time.

'Look happy,' I ordered. 'We're big buddies too, you and me. And if you even look suspicious I'll blast a hole in you.'

He nodded and I put the gun in my pocket. It looked bulky, and it looked like a gun in somebody's pocket, but in a place like the Peek-a-Boo nobody was going to get curious about it.

We got as far as the door, then somebody started banging on it. Vander looked at me quickly. I nodded and he called out:

'Who is it?'

'It's me, boss.'

The door opened and a small ferrety-looking character came bustling in. He had a face that was all points and ears that lay flat to his head. He wore a chocolate-coloured double-breasted suit with a yellow stripe shouting from the cloth. A yellow silk bow-tie and black and yellow patent leather shoes.

48

This guy was from Colourville. The large brown eyes became slits when he saw me.

'What do you want, Jammy, I'm busy right now,' Vander told him curtly.

Jammy nodded, curiosity bursting at the seams of his face.

'Yeah, sure thing, boss. It'll keep, I guess. But it is kind of important.'

When he came through the door he'd been full of news, his face had said that much. Now he was having to bottle it up, and the distillation of repressed news and unsatisfied curiosity about me was giving his emotions hell. And the way he kept his gaze rigidly diverted from my bulging pocket told me he'd read the situation.

'Be just a minute,' Vander said. 'Lola out there?'

'Lola?'

One thing this Jammy would never have made was an actor. His attempt to look nonchalant at the mention of Lola was comical. I wondered why. Wondered what was so important about Lola that made her different from the other half-dozen girls outside. I didn't have to wait long to find out.

'She ain't there, boss. That's what I come to tell you.'

Jammy shuffled his feet awkwardly. Vander stared at him.

'Whaddya mean she ain't there? You know what time it is? What kind of a deal is this?'

'It's kinda hard to explain, boss.'

Jammy rolled his eyes desperately at the club-owner, trying to signal that he didn't want to say too much in front of me. I shut the door and took the Police Special out of my pocket again. Waving it casually in Jammy's direction I said:

'Hard to explain? Does this make it any easier, Jammy?'

He gulped and did some more eye-rolling towards Vander, who nodded.

'Can't be much to it,' he advised the little man. 'Tell us both the story. Me and my friend here.'

The friend bit was an insult but I laughed it off. When you're the one with the gun you can afford a little laugh now and then. Jammy nodded, started to address Vander, then remembering the gun veered towards me. Finally, he settled for a point midway between us and talked at that.

'It's Lola,' he said slowly and distinctly. 'She's dead.'

'Dead?'

Vander and I said it together, but it was Vander who followed it up.

'How'd it happen?'

'Some kinda poison,' Jammy shrugged. 'They found her in that trap she lives in 'bout an hour ago.'

'They? You mean the cops?' I queried.

Jammy looked at me uncertainly before

replying. A quick jerk of the .38 made him certain.

'Er, no, not them. Some neighbours, or like that,' he stammered.

Vander chuckled.

'Well, well. That's tough about Lola. She wasn't a bad kid. But it leaves you back there with the Indians, huh? Try shoving that thing in Lola's face. It'll frighten her to death.'

The little guy in the loud suit just looked unhappy. He was clearly wishing his boss hadn't talked to me like that. It was not the tone to use when talking to a bad-tempered looking man who was pointing a heavy calibre automatic pistol at you. Guys that can be very unpredictable when upset, and like maybe blow somebody's head off. Somebody like Jammy's head for instance.

I ignored Vander and spoke to the frightened Jammy.

'And that's all you know about Lola?'

He nodded.

'Sure, mister, honest, I give you my word.'

I nodded back.

'I'll be around again,' I told him. 'Anything comes to mind about Lola you save it up real careful, and tell me next time I come.'

'You're wasting everybody's time,' Vander cut in. It was remarkable how confident he'd suddenly become since he heard about Lola's death. 'There's nothing here for you. Only one who might have known anything about Ruby

Capone was Lola, and she's dead. That's it.'

I looked at Jammy's face to see whether the mention of Ruby had brought any reaction, but there was nothing there.

'I'll be around just the same. Something might occur to you.'

'Something already occurred to me about what to do if you show round here again,' promised Vander quietly.

I went to the table, reached underneath and felt around for the wires leading to the button. My fingers located the thin cable and I pulled it clear and snapped it off. Vander watched this performance without expression, unlike Jammy whose eyes were popping out of his head.

'Over there.'

I motioned them both to the far wall. Jammy scuttled across fast. Vander moved more slowly, but he went. He was fairly confident by now that I wasn't going to shoot, but he also remembered what had happened to Took, and I'd had no need of a gun that time. Going to the door I opened it and put the .38 away.

'Everybody's been so friendly I forgot to tell you my name. It's Preston. Mark Preston.'

'I'll remember it,' promised Vander.

'I'll be back, Vander.'

He sneered and I didn't blame him. All I'd done was make a lot of noise and rough up one of his mugs. I hadn't got what I came after, in fact I hadn't got a single damned thing.

That was what he thought.

CHAPTER FOUR

Next morning I took a ride round to Police Headquarters. The *Globe* had carried the story about the death by poisoning of one Lola Wade. Lola had over-injected herself with heroin and the strong connection with Ruby Capone's death could not be ignored. There was an editorial about the evils of drug-taking, and a strong hint that there must be a current supply of heroin in the City which had been adulterated with some noxious chemical. Otherwise, asked the *Globe*, how could anyone explain how two separate addicts, each well aware of what constituted a fatal dose, should give themselves exactly that. Shad Steiner, the wily editor of the *Globe*, was a friend of mine who had strong views about drug pedlars. If I knew my man, he'd be mighty pleased with himself this morning. That editorial had probably set the heroin boys back a few hundred thousand dollars in the take. Your drug addict knows he's on a downhill slide to the morgue the whole time, but it's a gradual process. No amount of persuasion is going to deter him or her from following that inevitable

53

path. Steiner's editorial today was in a different class. It's one thing to know that each needle brings some vague future death a little nearer, quite another to wonder whether the current jab is equivalent to suicide.

I could imagine how Steiner would have rubbed his hands with glee when the idea for the editorial came to him. This was a heaven-sent opportunity to deal a real blow at the narcotics traffic. Of course, it meant that Shad had had to make a decision. For the story to have any impact, it had to be undiluted by other suggestions as to how these two more than coincidental deaths had come about. There was one obvious answer to that, and it was murder. The *Globe* was right on its main point. You don't get two B-girls, each presumably experienced in the administering of the big H, dying as a result of pumping in too much of the juice. Esecially when the two know each other and both work out of the same trap, the trap being the Peek-a-Boo Club. Steiner and the *Globe* had put their dollars on adulterated junk, but I liked murder better. One of the reasons for my call at Police Headquarters was to see if I could find out what they were betting on.

I knew the sergeant who had the desk duty, a square-built man by the name of Hagen. He inspected me quizzically.

'Who's on duty in Homicide today?' I queried.

Thoughtfully he laid down his ball point pen.

'Preston, isn't it?'

'It is.'

'You got any business with the boys upstairs?'

It looked like one of Hagen's difficult mornings.

'Maybe. Who knows?' I replied unco-operatively.

Hagen beamed.

'You do, Preston, you do. And if you're thinking of going upstairs you're going to have to tell me your little secret.'

'O.K.,' I said, trying to sound resigned. 'I have some information for Rourke.'

He looked severe.

'Would that be Lieutenant Rourke? Because, if it is, you'll have to watch your manners. Around here we like a little respect for a fine officer like that.'

'Sergeant Hagen,' I said wearily, 'do we have to go through this whole bit every time I come here? You know that I've known Rourke, all right, Lieutenant Rourke, since the flood. You know he'll see me, and you know I'm going to get up there in the end. So why all this performance every time?'

'Because I'm the duty sergeant, that's why. Because I'm supposed to find out people's business before I turn 'em loose in the building. As for knowing the lieutenant, a police officer with his record naturally meets every bum in town sooner or later.'

'All right, all right. Now do I get to go up? And you still haven't told me who has the duty up there.'

Hagen made a great show of thumbing through the duty roster that lay in front of him.

'The top squad. Lieutenant Rourke, Sergeant Randall, Detective Third Grade Schultz. And two other detectives, but we forgot to let 'em go home last night, so they're catching up on a little sleep this morning.'

'Thanks.'

I tramped up the worn stairs to the third floor. Considering the high incidence of murder in the annual criminal statistics, plus the equally high public outcry after each case, you would imagine both the authorities and the public would make it their business to provide some kind of facilities for the hard-worked Homicide Detail. Some kind of facilities would about describe the conditions under which Rourke and his men operated. They were allotted just three rooms on the third floor of the firetrap with the grand title of Monkton City Police Department Headquarters. Rourke and Randall shared a small room, there was a larger one next door for the squad of duty detectives. The third room was used for interrogations and was practically bare of furniture. There was also no rubber hose in the third room. Rourke didn't run his team that way.

I tapped at the dirty frosted glass with the word CAPTAIN stencilled on it in once-gold letters and opened the door. That's another thing about our generous civil authority. The homicide squad rates a Captain of Detectives, and Rourke has the job but not the rewards. He has to make it on a lieutenant's pay.

The iron-grey head was bent over a brown folder. The air was unpleasantly familiar with the stinging yellow fumes of the poisonous little Spanish cigars which were Rourke's special diet, of Randall there was no sign. I closed the door and waited for Rourke to lever his eyes up from the desk. It finally dawned on him somebody was standing there and he looked up at me without a change in his expression of concentration.

'Well, well,' he barked. 'You haven't got in my hair in months. I was beginning to figure you'd left town or something. Looks as if I'm going to be disappointed, huh?'

'How are you, John?'

'What kind of question is that? I'm busy, that's how I am. People in this town all seem to be hell-bent on getting themselves knocked off. Shootings, stabbings, poison. Last week we had a real ball. Some guy drowned his wife's boy-friend in a barrel of olive-oil. Cheered up the whole squad for days, a little variation like that.'

'Sounds like a whole heap of fun,' I replied

woodenly.

He wagged the grey head briskly.

'Well, what do you want this time?'

'You read the *Globe* yet today? Shad Steiner's lead on these heroin deaths?'

The fierce eyes narrowed.

'I read it. And?'

'And I wondered whether you agreed with what Shad said?'

'I thought it was a good story,' Rourke chewed on the nasty little black tube and a small cloud of acrid yellow smoke hung in front of his face. 'I don't always see eye to eye with Steiner, but he's given the junk-pushers a big headache this morning.'

'Yeah,' I agreed. 'But that isn't quite what I meant. Seems to me both these girls were users. Anybody can make a mistake, but two mistakes on two successive nights, this is quite an average. Just occurred to me there might be some other explanation. Like murder, for instance.'

He nodded. When you nod you bring your head forward, and Rourke's eyes were now in the centre of the poisonous smoke cloud. He didn't even blink.

'So it occurred to you. What makes it your business either way?'

'I'm looking for a bond-jumper,' I replied.

When you're in my line of business you get regular reports from a number of sources of matters that might come your way. A lot of it comes from the insurance companies, who are always interested in recovering stolen property, or tracing a bonded employee who went bad. I'd searched through these at the office before coming to see Rourke, and I'd come up with a case that would fit the circumstances. A forty-year-old bank official who'd taken a sack of the company's money and disappeared just over a year ago. With him he'd taken a girl, naturally. They nearly always do, and nearly always it isn't the girl they've been quietly married to for years. It was the girl who interested me. All I had was a vague general description, and it was vague enough and general enough to have fitted Ruby Capone. I told Rourke this tale.

'It's just a long shot,' I finished. 'Probably no connection. But there's a twenty-five hundred dollar reward so I thought it was worth a few hours' work. It's happened before, John. These guys are usually sick of the dame after a year. Even less.'

'Hm.'

It didn't mean he necessarily believed me. With Rourke you never knew what he believed. All it meant was what he said. H'm.

'Why didn't you come yesterday, if you're so interested in this Capone?' he asked suspiciously.

'Yesterday, I was only half-trying,' I replied. 'It seemed too remote a possibility. But when I asked around a few places I soon found out

59

nobody knew anything about Ruby Capone that went back as much as a year. She seems to have arrived from nowhere, the way these dames do. So I thought it was worth coming here to ask you.'

He nodded again, thinking about it.

'True enough about her history. She doesn't have any. Also she hasn't any police record, except here in Monkton, and that wasn't much. Well, I guess there's no harm in talking for a few minutes. Sit, if you want.'

I pulled up one of the battered wooden chairs and helped myself to an Old Favourite. The grey smoke looked puny as it curled up towards the ceiling.

'Been trying to bring it to mind, that bond-jumping you were speaking about. I have it now.' Rourke toyed with the black cheroot. 'Motor-cycle officer almost caught those two before they got properly started. They forced him off the road and into a wall. Quite a mess, I hear. The officer lost a leg. He was a very young man.'

'You have it, John,' I confirmed. 'That's the case I'm talking about.'

'Good, good. Now, this reward they posted. Two and a half thousand dollars I think you said. A great deal of money. How long will it take you to pick it up, if you get reasonable breaks?'

'Who knows? Not too long, if I get those breaks.'

'Plus,' he emphasised, 'a certain amount of co-operation from this department.'

'That too,' I acknowledged.

'You know how long an honest policeman has to work and risk his life for a sum like that?'

I was beginning to get the drift of the conversation, finally.

'Give it to me slowly, John,' I begged.

'You contribute five hundred to the Police Benefit, and you've got a deal,' he told me.

'This is corruption,' I protested fecbly.

'Words, words,' he shrugged. 'I'm a public official. You're just a private unofficial. You want co-operation you fatten up the Police Benefit. It'll only be a deduction from those high taxes you pay, anyway. Take it or leave it.'

'You sold me,' I gave in. 'Must have been the charming way you put it across.'

Rourke smiled broadly.

'I like a man like you, Preston. A private citizen who doesn't forget his debt to the Police Department. A guy who walks in here and offers to put a substantial sum in the Police Benefit. I can co-operate with somebody like that. What did you want to know?'

I looked concerned.

'Damned if I know. Hard to tell now what'll help and what won't. How about if you just tell me what you have?'

Rourke closed the brown folder, and took a

similar, thinner folder from a file tray.

'That won't take long,' he assured me. 'What I have in here wouldn't get a conviction against a vagrant. Let's see.'

He riffled through the thin sheets until his finger reached the one he wanted.

'Yup. This is it. Ruby Capone, white caucasian, height five feet six inches, weight one twenty, age approximately twenty-four—'

'Twenty-four?' I interrupted. 'Newspapers said twenty-seven.'

'Did you see the body?'

'No,' I admitted.

'Brother, she looked all of twenty-seven. Or thirty-seven for that matter. Anybody filling in quick details would make a mistake. That's why I always go for these lab. reports. With those guys it's for sure. If they say twenty-four that's my bet too.'

He waited to see if I had anything to offer. I hadn't.

'Dental work, minor only and good quality workmanship. Hair dark brown—and don't tell me what it said in the paper. These guys were looking at the roots. Eyes dark grey, complexion Mediterranean. You want to know what size girdle she wore?'

'No, thanks, not unless it comes up later. What was the cause of death?'

He looked up from the papers.

'Skipping the clinical details these guys have provided, she pumped enough heroin into her to kill a horse. Not in the arm though. Quite a few of the girls are getting wise to an old trick. They're shooting the juice into their thighs. This way they can wear sleeveless gowns without telling the whole wide world they're on the stuff. Cute, eh?'

'Very. Was she a known addict?'

'To us, you mean? No. But she would have been before long.'

He said this in a way that made my next question automatic.

'What do you mean by that?'

'I mean she'd been giving that needle plenty of action these past months.' Rourke tapped at the file. 'According to these figures here, she'd been spending something like a hundred a week on supplies, maybe more. When they get to that stage it isn't long before they put some business our way. It's simple, really. They need more money for the man than they can earn. In addition they're not working so hard as they ought to be, because of the effects of the junk. So they haven't got the price, but they must have a fix. What are they gonna do?'

I nodded.

'They have to go and take it away from somebody who has got it.'

'Correct. They try mugging somebody in an alley, or maybe they steal a car and try to knock over a filling station or a store. They're no good at it and we get a customer. Simple.'

'So you think the Capone girl was getting to

that stage?'

'Close to it, I'd guess,' he affirmed.

'How'd you think she came to die, John?'

He sighed and ran a hand like a catcher's mitt through the bristling grey hair.

'Yesterday you should have asked me that. Then I could have told you.'

'Let's pretend it's yesterday,' I offered. 'Why did she die?'

'Easy,' he pshawed. 'She has a big habit, right? Last night she was so desperate for a fix, so excited about what was coming, she didn't check properly. She just filled up that syringe and stuck it in her leg and pushed that plunger and kept on pushing. She was desperate, she didn't know what she was doing. Didn't care.'

I crushed out my cigarette in the tin ashtray, pushing aside the untidy heap of black stubs to find a space.

'Okay, that was yesterday. And today? What's your professional opinion today?'

'Huh.'

He sighed again and drummed on the table with enormous fingers.

'Well, now, today's a little different. Night before last I had a sudden death reported. Ruby Capone, a night-girl to put it kindly. Died from an overdose of heroin. Last night another sudden death. Lola Wade, another night-girl, also with a habit. Died from an overdose of heroin. Now we have two, and we have more than that. We have the fact that these two know each other, work around the same joint, one Peek-a-Boo Club. You might find some dumb Irish cop who would think it was all a great big coincidence. But it wouldn't be dumb Irish Rourke.'

'So what does he think?' I pressed.

'Don't know what the hell to think,' he groaned. 'Except it has to be murder. Don't ask me who or why, I don't know. If it was just the one girl I could think of a dozen reasons. Jealousy, hatred, blackmail, you name it. But two dames like that? What could they have in common that would justify knocking them off this way. I'm not saying they were harmless, especially Wade. Harmful would be a better description. But only to society generally. Not to one individual, one group.'

'How about the pushers?' I suggested.

Rourke looked at me with scorn.

'Where've you been lately? The pusher has nothing to fear from people like that. He's top dog, the man. The one with the happy dust. Whatever he wants, they'll see he gets it. No, no. Not the man.'

'Could they be witnesses to something?' I tried.

'Sure. Certainly they could. In fact I'd bet on it. If I knew half what they'd witnessed, I could close a few files around this department. But who're they going to tell? The law? They'd know what would happen to them if they did. Plus, we don't supply any junk in the cells, and that's where they'd have to go, for their own protection.'

He blinked, yawned and looked at me.

'Forgot to tell you something. Capone didn't die in that rat-trap apartment of hers.'

If I was listening before, I was sitting on the edge of my seat now.

'Where, then?'

'We don't know yet. Just that she'd been dead an hour or two when she was dumped at the Villa Marina. I have a theory about it, but it isn't any more than that. I'm working on the idea that she could have died somewhere that wasn't convenient to somebody. Especially somebody in the narcotics trade. She could have been with him when she gave herself the fix, and instead of having himself a ball he suddenly found he had a stiff on his hands. You go and quote me to anybody I'll break your leg. But it isn't a bad idea. It's been done before.'

I agreed. Practically anybody with a police record would have an attack of the jumping heebies at the prospect of explaining to the law how he came to have a dead girl on his hands.

'What about the other one, Lola Wade? Anything unusual there?'

'No. She was dressed ready for bed when she died. Of course, I'm not saying there wasn't somebody with her at the time.'

I said gently:

'In fact, there would have needed to be if

66

she was murdered.'

Rourke snorted.

'Not necessarily. This fatal dose didn't have to be administered by anybody else. It was double strength stuff. Could have been supplied to her by anybody over the past week or so. It's not at all impossible, if there was somebody with her when she died, he could have been as innocent as you or me.'

None of which seemed to be getting us any further forward.

'Well, outside of any connection we can establish between these two, I'm not especially interested in Lola Wade. Ruby Capone is the one who could be my bail-jumper's girl friend. What have you dug up on her?'

Rourke looked at me with that knowing pity which was so terrifying to the younger members of his department.

'You know what she was, where she operated. What would you expect me to dig up? She lived in a rathole called the Villa Marina. She was very respectable and quiet. Everybody at the Villa Marina says so. In fact, everybody at the Villa Marina is respectable and quiet. In the past two years we have removed one army deserter, a rapist and two known prostitutes from the Villa Marina. But everybody there tells me everybody else is respectable and quiet. Then there's the place of work, if I could use the term. An innocent little place of amusement called the Peek-a-

Boo Club. Run by a fringe character named Vander—Max Vander's brother by the way. You remember Max, the one they called the laughing assassin? So there's good blood there for a beginning. Vander runs a respectable place, no trouble with the law. Capone hustled drinks for him on percentage. No, sir, lieutenant, none of his girls would go in for any of that other stuff. Did Capone have any special friends? Oh yes, certainly. There was a big guy, whose name was Ed, or was it Charlie? Anyway, he was one. There was another one, a sailor. He had a moustache and looked kind of foreign. No, we never did know his name. And a couple of other guys with no names whom we couldn't describe, lieutenant. Sure, Capone had lots of friends. No, none of them around right now, but if any of them come in, we'll be sure and have them call you. Don't mention it, always glad to co-operate with the police.'

I grinned at the despair in Rourke's voice. He'd been through the same routine so many times he knew the dialogue by heart, in advance.

'Some day,' said Rourke reflectively, 'I'm going to get a real fat murder case, and I'm going to know just who the people are who could help me with it. Then I'm going to the Commissioner and turn in my badge. After that, I'm going to call on all those people, one at a time, and kind of persuade them into telling me a few little items of information. I once worked it out on paper. If I could dodge the members of my own department, who would naturally be trying to pick me up to stop me getting any more information, I reckon I could probably solve a straightforward case of homicide inside twenty-four hours.'

The dream. The dream of every law-enforcement officer I'd ever known. Twenty-four hours with a free hand, or more accurately, in which to get free with their hands. It would never be allowed of course. Too many people would find the mud sticking. But it was a beautiful dream, and it didn't cost the taxpayers a cent.

'Tell me about the immorality rap that you grabbed Capone for last month. According to the *Globe*, that is.'

'Oh, that? We hadn't really got anything that would stick. Just thought it would make Vander watch his step for a while. There were three girls mixed up in it. They all got off. Wade was one of the others, and a lulu name of Schwartz. Rose Schwartz. They both have a name for being respectable and quiet too. Or had, I should say, in Wade's case.'

'The paper said Capone was going to sue the city,' I continued. 'Anything in that, John?'

He shook the grizzled head.

'Nah. Or if there was, it certainly hasn't come my way yet. And I'd be the first one roasted.'

I got up to leave.

'Well, this seems to be a cold deck I'm holding. Your boys can't trace any connection of Ruby Capone's, so I'm sure I can't. That doesn't mean she wasn't the girl I'm after. But it seems to indicate she wasn't in touch with my man of recent weeks at least. Even if she was the one, I'm inclined to think the guy dumped her and took off alone. Which puts me right back where I started.'

He toyed with a pencil. In his hands it looked like a match.

'You gonna leave this one be?' he asked curiously.

'No,' I replied. 'I'll chew on it a while, maybe ask a few more questions here and there. For twenty-five hundred dollars I can spare a few hours of my working time.'

'Two thousand dollars,' he corrected. 'You already promised the five hundred.'

'It comes to mind,' I assured him. 'If you pick up anything will you tip me off?'

'Maybe. If it doesn't mean breaking procedure. Yeah, I guess so.'

I thanked him and left. Monkton City didn't seem to know much about Ruby Capone. I wondered whether I might give Ruby a miss for a while, and spend some time on Jeannie Benson.

CHAPTER FIVE

The morning smog was thinning as I left the city and soon I was out on the highway, heading out into the split-level territory. The strengthening sun was warming up the air, and I was glad to roll down the windows after a mile or two. I was making for Vale City where one Jeannie Benson had once lived and worked. Vale had once been a huddle of shacks, acting as a stopover for pioneers heading for the coast. Just sixteen miles short of their ultimate destination, they got into a habit of resting at Vale for maybe a day and a night before completing the journey. The time would be spent in getting themselves and their equipment cleaned up and polished, so they could finish the trip in something like style. Vale had a wheelwright and a blacksmith, a general store and a place where a lady could take a bath in comfort. It was the bath that really sold the women, after days and weeks of hot dry tramping, with barely enough water to drink, leave alone bathing. Also there was no saloon. The guys who ran Vale back in those days must have had keen senses of perception. A saloon would have been a mistake. After the hardships and dangers of the overland trek, the men could have been excused for wanting to let down when they came to their first saloon in hundreds of miles. But that would have brought the gamblers, the gals and the gunfighters. The town would quickly get a bad name, and the wagon trains would take a two or three mile detour to avoid the place. So, no saloon and plenty of legitimate business.

Times change. The strait-laced business men of oldtime Vale would have been surprised at the way their town had developed. The no-saloon tradition lasted nearly half-a-century which was quite a tribute to the original inhabitants, but with the end of World War I a little development called prohibition tipped over the apples. And Vale went wild, even wilder than most other towns its size. Fifty years of enforced abstention seemed to have built up the most almighty thirst among the good people of Vale City, and they set about assuaging it with a vigour and flourish that would have been a great asset to any more notable endeavour. Unofficial figures indicated that the consumption of proof alcohol and beer was eighteen points higher, per man, woman and child of the Vale population, than the average for the whole country. Prohibition finished thirty years ago, but the number of bars in Vale City was still out of proportion to its population.

It was almost noon as I rolled into the heart of town. I was looking for an address on Wheelwright Avenue, so-named because of the site of the original wheelwright's stables.

Idly I wondered whether anybody else in that busy traffic-stream was giving a thought to that old-time craftsman as they bustled along between the towering concrete piles. Dawdling along by the kerb I finally located the particular pile I was looking for, parked and got out.

The Handford Construction Company was on the eighth floor. I suffered a silent ride with a gloomy and aged elevator man. At eight I entered a long narrow passageway, and walked along looking for the Handford set-up. The company occupied almost two-thirds of the eighth level and it wasn't hard to find. I opened the door marked 'enquiries' and went up to a black-topped desk. Here sat a middle-aged woman of stern appearance who was obviously determined that nobody was going to get past her too easily, and maybe waste the time of the Handford Construction Company.

I smiled engagingly and she stared back stonily.

'Like to see Mr. Handford, please.'

'Have you an appointment?' she demanded.

'Well no, but—'

She held up a hand for silence. I was silent.

'I'm extremely sorry. Nobody gets in to see Mr. Handford without an appointment. I might be able to get you a few minutes with one of our senior executives.'

She lifted an enquiring eyebrow, to see how I reacted to this magnanimous offer.

'No, it has to be Mr. Handford,' I said regretfully. 'This is a personal matter, not business.'

For the first time I detected the slightest gleam of interest.

'Oh, I see. You are a friend of Mr. Handford's, then?'

'No, I've never met him—'

Up went the hand again and I stopped talking again.

'Then it's quite out of the question. Mr. Handford never—'

'We've been all through that, lady,' I interrupted. 'Do you have an envelope?'

She was so surprised at being interrupted that she turned almost automatically to retrieve an envelope from some hidden place beside her desk. She laid it in front of me without a word. Trying to look mysterious, I took a card from my pocket, wrote on the back 'This will only take five minutes, Mr. Handford,' slipped the card into the envelope and sealed it down. Then, very carefully, I wrote his full name, 'Walter F. Handford,' on the front. Almost as an afterthought I added, 'Personal and Confidential', then handed the envelope back to the sentry.

'Have this taken to him, please. I'll wait.'

She stared at the sealed oblong suspiciously. Then she called over her shoulder:

'George.'

A young boy with crew-cut hair materialised

74

behind her.

'Ma'am?'

'Take this along to Mr. Handford's office and give it to his personal secretary.' The 'personal' was underlined. 'There'll be no need to wait for an answer.'

This done, she turned back to me with a slight smirk. She didn't know what I'd written on that card, but she wasn't worried. What she did know was that Mr. Handford never saw anybody without an appointment. And if I thought a few scribbled words on a piece of pasteboard—

The buzzer on her desk sounded. She flicked a key.

'Enquiries.'

A girl's voice said:

'Do you have a Mr. Preston waiting there?'

I nodded to indicate I was Preston.

'Why, yes,' said my enemy, flustered.

'Have George bring him along, please. Mr. Handford will see him.'

With icy calm she broke the connection, and said over her shoulder:

'George.'

'Yes, ma'am.'

George did his rapid appearing act again.

'Take this gentleman to see Mr. Handford.'

In turning back she contrived not to look at me again. I decided she didn't want to risk remembering my face. It might haunt her at nights, the face of the creature who got in to see Mr. Handford without an appointment. That kind of thing can disturb the balance of the mind.

'This way, sir.'

I followed the cheerful-looking George past a few rows of desks, all occupied by people too busy with their work to look up. Construction seemed to be the thing to buy, if this office was any indication.

George knocked gently at a door, opened it and waved me in. I suppose I'd been expecting another gorgon and when I saw what I saw I did a double-take. She had red hair, a soft chestnut colour, falling straight to a rolled bob under the ears. This is supposed to be out of date. Anybody who thinks so hasn't stood where I was standing. High cheekbones, a retroussé nose, and a mouth rather larger than perfect symmetry would have required. That was symmetry, not me. With me she was perfect as she was. The green eyes matched the tailored light-weight suit with a dipped front. Her throat was like rich cream.

'Mr. Preston?'

The voice was light and musical. Friendly, too, or maybe I just wanted to think so. I nodded.

'If you're Walter F. Handford, somebody made a mistake,' I grinned.

She smiled, not too much.

'I'm Paula Brickman, the last obstacle before anyone sees Mr. Handford.'

And what a hurdle, I reflected.

'In that case, I'm sorry. I can only talk to Mr. Handford in person.'

The rolled hair swung lazily as she nodded her head.

'He's going to give you a moment. He has a long-distance telephone call, but he's almost through.'

'Thank you.'

I stood there, trying not to look like a starving wolf viewing a shorn lamb.

'Excuse me if I seem to be staring,' she said, 'but I've never seen a private investigator before.'

This was my big chance and I wasn't going to miss it. I opened my mouth to deliver a fair sample of my best private investigator conversation when an amber light flashed on the ivory telephone by her hand.

'Mr. Handford has finished his call,' she told me. 'You may go in now.'

I didn't want to go in. Handford was of no interest. What I wanted was to spend whatever time was necessary in giving myself a king-sized build-up with this gorgeous creature. That was what I wanted. What I did was to nod my thanks, cross the room and open the door marked 'Private'.

Walter F. Handford rose from the gun-metal desk to hold out his hand. I already knew he was about forty. Now I found he was also tall, with an easy good-natured face and a body in hard, physical shape. He shook briefly and invited me to sit.

'Don't mind telling you, Mr. Preston, I'm relieved you're here.'

Well, that was the darnedest opening speech. Then he went on:

'Yes, I must say I'm relieved. After all, I've only had the thing a few weeks, and I wasn't looking forward to explaining to the insurance company. Smoke?'

He held out a sandalwood box, and I took a cigarette and lit both his and mine. He exhaled luxuriously.

'Ah,' he breathed. 'Now let's get on. Where exactly did you find it?'

It was my turn to talk at last.

'Find what? I haven't found anything, Mr. Handford.'

Some of the good humour dissipated. Not all.

'Haven't found it? Now, wait. Just wait one little minute. You have come about my car, haven't you?'

'No, sir, I have not,' I admitted. 'Is it lost?'

'Lost? Stolen. Stolen from right outside City Hall, while I was at a council meeting.' His face and voice clearly indicated his disappointment. 'I was sure that was what you'd come about. Ah, well. That's enough about that. Just why are you here, Mr. Preston?'

I tapped ash into a silver bowl on the desk.

'I'm trying to locate somebody who seems to be missing, Mr. Handford. A young lady who was last heard of here in Vale City, several months back. Her name is Jeannie Benson.'

His face changed at the mention of the name. There was something in his eyes, sadness perhaps.

'Ah, yes, Jeannie. And why have you come to me?'

'Because you were a friend of hers, and might have some idea where she went,' I said frankly.

He held a hand up to his face and pulled absent-mindedly at an ear.

'Who told you I was a friend of hers?'

His tone wasn't suggesting that what I said wasn't true. He merely wanted to know where I got my information. I smiled my honest smile.

'Practically half the people in town,' I returned. 'After all, you hardly made a secret of it, did you?'

He shook his head, and smiled reminiscently.

'I guess that's true enough. Mr. Preston, as you say, Jeannie was a friend of mine. A very dear friend. You, by contrast, are a total stranger. You understand I don't intend to sound offensive, but what has my friendship with Jeannie Benson to do with you?'

I looked serious again.

'That's a fair question. As you saw from the

card, I'm a private investigator. Some of the time I work for the insurance companies. One of them had a substantial life cover on Miss Benson. The premiums were always paid when due, have been for years. Then suddenly the payments ceased. This is not uncommon, and there's usually quite a simple explanation. But sometimes it doesn't seem so simple and Miss Benson's case is in that category. In fact, there doesn't seem to be a trace of her.'

'I see.'

He got up suddenly, walked to the window and stared down at the traffic stream a hundred feet below.

'I don't quite follow this,' he said, after a few moments. 'Surely the man who should be asking me questions is the local manager of the insurance company. Why should they incur the additional expense of hiring you? And I believe it can be quite an expense.'

I was ready for that one, too.

'Normally, yes. But this policy wasn't covered by the local office. It was dealt with from the start at the company's head office, in San Francisco. It's something to do with company protocol. Since the local man has never had a percentage of the gravy, it is the policy of the company not to call him in when things look like getting, shall we say, irregular. That's when the head office hires somebody like me. It's cheaper than sending out one of their own investigators all the way from San

Francisco. Especially since these things are usually explained quite easily, and most of 'em turn out to be a wild goose chase anyway.'

It sounded convincing, but I didn't swell with pride over the fact. What I'd told Handford was an established procedure with one or two of the bigger companies, so it had every right to sound authentic.

Handford nodded, as if satisfied. I had an impression that he wasn't keen to talk about Jeannie Benson, either to me or anybody else. If what her father had told me was correct, and if in fact there had been talk of marriage between these two, I could understand how this man would feel.

'I'll tell you anything I can.'

'Thank you, Mr. Handford. I realise that I might be intruding in your personal life, but believe me, my only interest is in locating Miss Benson. Now, the last premium was paid six months ago. Payments were due at two-monthly intervals, and so there are now three outstanding. I'm telling you this so you'll have the whole background. With this kind of policy, it is only after three premiums have not been paid, that the company takes this step.'

'Go on.'

'Well, sir,' I spread my hands in a gesture of frankness, 'candidly I have nothing else. She worked in this town, she lived here. There was nothing abnormal about her activities so far as I can judge. And yet, starting six months ago, it's as though she never existed.'

'But this is hardly rare, is it? I mean, the papers carry similar stories every day of the week. A girl has a row with her family, or she gets dismissed from her job, or something quite ordinary like that. Then something prompts her to go off somewhere and try to start her life again.'

It was my turn to nod.

'Absolutely correct, Mr. Handford. Absolutely. And I've been hoping from the start that I would find something like that had happened here. In fact, if you know that it was something like that, please tell me about it, and I'll be on my way, perfectly satisfied.'

Handford looked at me hard, and there was no expression on his face to give me any lead to his thoughts. Then he came slowly back to his chair and sat down. Wearily, he passed a hand over his face. Then he sighed, and said:

'Wish I could, Preston. Oh, how I wish that. I don't mind telling you that your visit here is quite a shock to me. When Jeannie ran away— yes, I know about that and I'll tell you the whole thing, in a moment—when she went I thought I'd be sure to hear from her sometime. In fact I didn't. Never heard a word about her since then. Until now, of course. It's quite a shock.'

'In what way, a shock?' I queried.

He smiled, faintly.

'By asking that, you certainly show how little

you know about Jeannie. Apart from her other wonderful qualities, she was one of the most methodical persons I've ever known. Her personal affairs were always tidy, to put it mildly. She was one of these people, if she was expecting an account from one of the stores in town and it was late coming, she'd call up the store and ask where it was. She was, what's the word I want, scrupulous. Yes, in money matters Jeannie was scrupulous. She would never let anything so important as an insurance premium get neglected. If she's failed to pay three consecutive premiums it can only mean she's ill somewhere, terribly ill. That's what I mean by a shock. And that's why I'm going to do my damnedest to help you find her. She may need help, poor kid.'

'Thank you,' I acknowledged. 'You mentioned something about her running away?'

He looked mournful.

'Yes. Well, I might as well tell you about that. I've never told anyone here in Vale about it. Maybe it won't be so bad, telling it to a complete stranger.'

'That's sometimes easier,' I agreed.

'I first met Jeannie Benson a little more than two years ago. She was very attractive, and I mean that in a nice way. Jeannie knew how to wear clothes and make her hair pretty, in a way that made you want to stare at her, and yet at the same time you could tell she wasn't, what shall I say, cheap. She was very self-possessed too, without being boring about it. Jeannie had read a lot, could talk on a dozen subjects with some authority. Well, I dated her a few times, then it got to be a recognised thing that she was my date. If either of us was asked anywhere, the other was invited automatically. You know the kind of situation.'

I indicated that I knew the kind of situation.

'I was fifteen years older than she, but that didn't make any difference. In fact it was almost necessary. She was so mature in her outlook and everything that she made these young fellows her own age look like schoolkids. No, the age difference wasn't significant.'

He looked at me anxiously to see whether I was showing any disapproval. It was obvious from the careful way he'd spoken about their ages that this was a subject he'd given a lot of thought in the past. I didn't register anything else but interest.

'For quite a while I hadn't any serious interest in her. She was lively and intelligent company, a girl you could introduce into almost any surroundings and she'd know how to conduct herself. More than that wasn't in my mind for a long time, several months.'

'And then you found you were getting attached to her?'

'Yes. I began to realise I was spending a lot

84

of time thinking about her and, well, next thing I knew, we were in love.'

He turned his face away as he said it. Stranger or no, love is not something you go around talking about. Not most men anyway, certainly not Walter F. Handford.

'I appreciate how difficult this is, Mr. Handford,' I assured him. 'Please don't bother to tell me any more about that side of it. Let's get to the time Miss Benson left town.'

He shook his head.

'No, no, I have to tell you all of it. You see, I hadn't any right to fall in love with anybody. I'm already married.'

Till he said that, I'd been working up quite a sympathy for him. The sympathy curve took a sudden dive. Carefully I said:

'I don't think I quite follow. If you were seeing so much of Miss Benson, and to use your own words, people in this town thought of you as a twosome, you presumably live apart from your wife?'

He laughed ironically.

'Oh, you could say that. Very much apart. For the past twelve years my wife has been in a home for the mentally incurable.'

And that made it a lot plainer.

'I'm sorry,' I said. I meant it.

Handford shrugged.

'You're sorry. Everybody's sorry. But that doesn't help me much. It didn't prevent me losing Jeannie.'

'The laws are quite sympathetic to cases of this kind these days,' I offered tentatively.

Handford replied seriously.

'It depends on what you mean by the laws. If you're talking about the laws of this state, or of the country for that matter, you're probably right. But there are older laws than these. Laws of human behaviour, Preston. It may sound kind of old-fashioned in this lovely plastic age, but there are such things as the laws of humanity. I can't just divorce Sarah, pretend she never happened. Because she did happen, she was my wife and I loved her very dearly before—before she had to go away. And that's not the end of it. You may be interested to know why she's in that place? I'll tell you. Because she was hurt in an automobile smash, being driven too fast by a drunken fool. I was that driver, and it's my fault she's where she is. Nobody's else's.'

Some people have an awful lot to live with. Handford seemed to be one of them. He'd have to be carrying around a guilt complex a mile high after a thing like that. I could have argued with him if it had been any business of mine. I could have rationalised and theorised and all the rest of the -iseds. So could most people. Most people could tell Walter Handford that he had to get on with his own life, that making himself and Jeannie Benson miserable wasn't going to do one thing towards improving Sarah Handford's mental condition.

They could say he'd suffered enough, after twelve years of enforced loneliness. Only it wasn't their business, and it wasn't mine. The man whose business it was, sat facing me across the desk, and he was the only one who had any right to an opinion about his own private hell.

'You said Mrs. Handford is in a home for the mentally incurable,' I reminded him.

'Yes, the House of Calm, about ten miles from town,' he replied. 'Why?'

'Does it mean that there is no hope of eventual recovery?'

He shook his head.

'No. That's the part that puts me in this position. I haven't found a single doctor who'll state definitely that Sarah will never recover. In fact, she has odd periods of lucidity from time to time. That's why I've got to stay married to her. I've robbed her of twelve years of her life through my swinish drunkenness. If there's any chance, no matter how remote, that she may ever be cured, I'll be waiting. I owe her that.'

That made sense. A tough hard-to-take kind of sense. Handford was a man with a lot of old-fashioned guts.

'Thank you for telling me this,' I said. 'I think it explains what happened between you and Miss Benson.'

'It does. We got in deeper and deeper. After all, we weren't children. We were two adult

87

people, and we were—well—trapped, for want of a better word. We kept on saying we'd stop seeing each other, that it would never work out. But we didn't mean it, not really. A couple of days was the longest we ever managed to stay apart. I can't tell you whether any particular incident finally drove her away. I've thought about it a thousand times. I guess she just sat down that day and thought it all out rationally. We could never keep away from each other while we stayed in the same town. I couldn't easily leave, because my business is here. Jeannie must have decided if we were ever going to break up, it was up to her. So she just walked out. I've never heard a word from her.'

'This question probably sounds kind of unnecessary, Mr. Handford, but I have to ask,' I told him. 'Could you give me the slightest idea of where she could have gone? Any old friends or family that she may have mentioned at some time? Even a town might help.'

I knew it would be a waste of time asking. Handford wasn't the type not to have done something about it if he'd had a lead to Jeannie. He shook his head, predictably.

'No. She had no family, they died when she was small. They'd left her well provided for, and she actually grew up in a convent somewhere in the north of the state. I don't know exactly where, but I imagine a big insurance company could probably find out if

88

they really wanted to know. After all, how many convents are there which would have brought up an orphan by that name?'

'True enough,' I conceded. 'If the company want to pursue that, I've no doubt they could trace the convent. But I can't think we're liable to have any need to follow that particular enquiry. We're not concerned so much with where she's been in the past, as where she is now. Any other place she might return to, but the convent I'd doubt.'

Handford looked at me searchingly to see whether there was any double meaning to my last remark. There wasn't.

'So where will you go from here?' he asked.

'I don't know,' I confessed. 'Not much for me in this town, I'd say. Did Miss Benson have a girl-friend, you know, somebody she might confide in?'

'I've thought of that before. Months ago. There's nothing to learn, take my word.'

'Just the same,' I pressed gently, 'if there is such a girl I'd like to meet her, just have a talk. Even general impressions can help. And you would be surprised, Mr. Handford, at the different picture a woman will give of another woman, compared with the way a man sees her.'

He gave in.

'Why of course, if you really think it could help. There is a girl. Her name is Francie, Francie Andrews. She and Jeannie used to share an apartment one time. Then I came into the picture, and Francie went back to live with her family. It was only an experiment anyway, her living away from home. I think she was glad to have a solid excuse for getting back to some regular meals.'

He grinned, I grinned back.

'I'll write her address down. Here.'

He scribbled quickly on a blue note-pad and tore off the sheet.

'It's north side of town. Go straight on up Main, take a right turn at the pioneer memorial and then ask again.'

I looked at the address, folded the sheet and slipped it in my pocket. Then I got up to leave.

'Thanks for all the co-operation, Mr. Handford.'

We shook hands again. He said:

'You could do something for me if you would.'

'Surely,' I returned. 'What is it?'

'If you find out anything about her, about Jeannie, let me know. Would you do that?'

I nodded.

'Pleasure. I'll do better. Give you a call over the weekend in any case. Let you know how I'm making out.'

'Fine. Thanks a lot.'

I was glad to be getting out of his office. My presence there wasn't doing anything to help him forget about Jeannie Benson. Some people attract trouble like flies and Handford seemed to be in that category. Now he could sit around a while and hope against his better judgment that everything was all right with Jeannie. And I'd have the sweet problem of trying to decide how much I ought to tell him. Not because of the instructions my client had given me. More because of Jeannie herself. It was for me to decide whether or not she would want Handford to know. I shrugged the thought away. After all, that wasn't for decision today. I'd worry about it later.

In the outer office the cherry-coloured head swung in my direction.

'All through, Mr. Preston?'

'All through, honey. Look, I may never have to come and see Mr. Handford again, but there's no reason why you and I should part forever, is there?'

She grinned and it made me feel warmer all over.

'A reason? Yes, I know one. Six feet three, two hundred and ten pounds of bad-tempered reason. A ball-player, who has sort of taken it into his head that my free time belongs to him.'

'It's a democracy, honey. Women are allowed to vote nowadays. Even have opinions. I'm not interested in what he thinks you should do with your free time. Let's have your opinion.'

She sighed.

'I'm afraid I agree with him. Look.' She held

up her left hand and the sunlight danced redly from the stone on her third finger.

Suddenly the atmosphere was chillier than I'd thought.

'He's a lucky ball-player,' I told her. 'It was a good idea, just the same.'

A few minutes later I was back in the Chev, and heading up Main as instructed.

CHAPTER SIX

The Andrews' house was one of a whole row of what looked like a vet development. Many of the other houses were running down, and successive owners had held such a variety of views about what constituted a design for living in that it was difficult to imagine back to the time when all these houses were identical. Certainly the trimmest property on view was the one I'd come to visit. I walked up the narrow path, between rows of whitened sea-shell, carefully cemented into a border. The bright green paintwork of the porch was fresh and cheerful. The Andrews evidently were believers in making a home look like a home.

There was an old-fashioned bell-pull, which slid out smoothly as I yanked on it. A mellow boom sounded from inside, and a woman's voice called out to somebody else. I didn't catch the words.

The door opened, and a little round woman with a lively face looked me up and down.

'I'm calling on Miss Andrews, Miss Francie Andrews. Is she home, please?'

She decided I was not a thug on the run and opened the door wider.

'She's here. Better come on in out of the sun. I'll call her.'

I stepped into a cheerful hall and Mrs. Andrews closed the door.

'I'm her mother,' she announced, holding out her hand.

'Oh, Preston is my name,' I replied, shaking hands. 'Mark Preston.'

'Uh, huh. Glad to know you.'

She went to the foot of the stairs and called up.

'Francie, friend of yours is here. A Mr. Preston.'

A muffled cry came from above. It could have been the word 'who?'.

Mrs. Andrews was not going to spend all day, yelling up and down stairs.

'You come on down and you'll find out.'

She turned to me and smiled widely.

'That'll fetch her faster'n a flea. Francie never could bear not to know who was here.'

'Thank you very much.'

She nodded and walked away towards the back of the house. As she went through a door at the rear a brown-haired boy in his late teens passed her and came up to me.

'I'm Hec,' he announced. 'I'm her big brother. You're calling on Francie, that right?'

I nodded.

'Hallo.'

'Hallo yourself.'

He tucked his thumb into well-worn jeans, rocking back and forth on his heels.

'You're kind of old for my sister, ain't you? Did you know she's only twenty-two years old?'

I didn't know how I'd got into this in the first place. These people would have a preacher round if I stayed much longer. Anyway the kid annoyed me. If Walter Handford wasn't too old for the Benson girl, I didn't see why I shouldn't qualify for Francie Andrews. Then I realised I was catching it, too. Something about the atmosphere. Before I could reply to Hec Andrews there was the sound of someone coming downstairs. I looked up to catch my first sight of Francie.

The first thing to come into view was a white shoe with a very look-attable ankle just above. Then long, slender legs, the muscles of her calves thrown into relief with each downward step. All too soon, a crisp white linen skirt, topped off with sunburst blouse against which the points of her breasts jogged restlessly. Her throat was a smooth light olive colour, merging into the strong lines of her jaw. Francie Andrews had a pear-shaped face, accentuated by that firm jaw-line. Her eyes were dark, and her nose wide-set above a cruel red slash of a mouth. The hair was black, cut short and almost straight. She wasn't beautiful, but she was striking, very definitely.

Her careful descent of the stairs had been a staged entrance for whoever constituted the audience. I constituted the audience and I would have applauded gladly if Hec hadn't been still there, rocking about aggressively, and trying to look like a character from West Side Story. Francie was at the foot of the stairs now, staring at me coolly. Then her eyes flickered towards her brother with impatience.

'Hec, scram.'

He hesitated, looked me over to remind me the Jets never forget, then kicked at the floor and walked away.

'We'll go in here,' she said to me, and led me into a small room beside the stairs.

When we were in, she closed the door firmly.

'I chose this room because it's the only room in the house where you can talk without anybody hearing from the other side of the door. I had to find out by bitter experience when my first dates started to call. Hec is always listening. Shall we sit down?' She was tall, about five-eight was my guess, and she wore some delicate perfume that was playing the devil with my senses. We sat down and I wondered how long it would be before it occurred to this self-possessed girl to ask who I was and what I was doing there.

While I was wondering that, I was also staring hard at her legs where the linen skirt had fallen back from her knees as she sat. She made a not very convincing attempt to pull it down a little.

'I know who I am, and I'm sure you do, otherwise you wouldn't be here,' she told me. 'Could I know who you are, now?'

I told her my name, and that I was from Monkton City. She nodded.

'It's about Jeannie Benson, isn't it? You've come to talk to me about her.'

She said it quite matter-of-factly, as though she also did a little water-divining on the side. It took me aback.

'Why should I be here about Jeannie Benson?' I queried.

'Aren't you?'

I shook my head.

'I asked you first.'

She smoothed at the skirt again, and I resolved not to look in that direction any more.

'You're a stranger. No stranger ever called at this house to see me in my whole life. Plenty of men, but no strangers. Plenty of strangers, but not calling on me. So it has to be about something unusual. And the only really unusual part of my life is Jeannie Benson.'

'Doesn't sound very convincing,' I suggested. 'I can think of half-a-dozen things that might bring a stranger to see you.'

'No,' she contradicted flatly. 'Besides, I've always worried about her, ever since she ran off. Always had this fear that some day, somebody would come and tell me something awful had happened to her.'

'I see.'

I dug around in my pockets, produced a pack of Old Favourites.

'Mind if I smoke?'

'Not if I can join you.'

We lit cigarettes and took up the time having a good look at each other.

'Are you police?' she asked.

'No. I'm what they call a private investigator. You've heard it before?'

'I've heard it before,' she confirmed. 'What are you investigating?'

'Why should anything awful happen to Miss Benson?' I countered.

She threw back her head to puff smoke towards the ceiling. As she did so her breasts jutted sharply against the silk blouse. The manoeuvre didn't strike me as accidental.

'Jeannie was a girl with trouble in her life before she ever came to Vale City,' said Francie slowly.

'Trouble? What kind of trouble?'

'I don't know. She never would tell me a thing about it. Not a thing, in all that time we lived together. That takes quite some doing, when you have two girls living in each other's pockets. That's how I could tell it was real, deep trouble. If it had been anything less, like a broken romance or something like that, she'd have told me the whole story within a month.'

I nodded while I pondered that interesting fragment of female psychology.

'O.K. I buy that. But why should that mean anything awful has happened to her now?'

'You ever meet her?' she asked.

'No.'

'You seem like a shrewd kind of man. Have to be, I guess, in your business. If you'd met Jeannie you'd have sensed the trouble around her. She was like somebody who knew things could never really work out for them, that something would always interfere. Something bad.'

I didn't know Francie Andrews, so it wasn't easy to evaluate what she was telling me. It sounded like a compound of many things. A backward character assessment of the Benson girl, based not so much on impressions gathered at the time as on the sum of those impressions studied at leisure in the period which had passed since Jeannie disappeared. Plus perhaps one or two pieces of information assimilated during a couple of lectures at high school. All stirred together with the great movie tradition of the *femme fatale*, now served in the watered-down version on the little glass box at regular intervals.

Francie Andrews was a girl with an interesting line in conversation. To say nothing of certain other interesting lines, interrupted from time to time by bumps and curves, at which I was definitely not going to stare again during this interview.

'Has something happened to her?' she asked abruptly.

'I don't know,' I lied. 'I'm trying to find her.'

'Why?'

'Does it matter?'

'It does to me. I'm a friend of hers. As I've told you, Jeannie had something bad in her past. How do I know you're not that something? How do I know you're not looking for her just to drag her back to that past of hers, whatever it was?'

It was a reasonable question. I did my act about the insurance cover again, and it seemed to satisfy her. When I was through she nodded seriously.

'You're absolutely right. Something has to be wrong for Jeannie to be late with her payments. She believes in paying what she owes, and promptly. Still, I don't see how I can help you. I last saw her about two days before she left town and I haven't seen hide nor hair of her since.'

Although that was what I'd been expecting, I still felt a slight disappointment.

'How did she seem, that last time?'

Francie frowned and tapped at the unlit end

99

of her cigarette with an impatient thumb.

'Quite normal,' she replied.

'How would she be when she was normal?' I pressed.

'Oh, sort of friendly. She had a wonderful disposition you know. Always ready to talk, and she'd make witty remarks. Jeannie had a great sense of humour. Not the back-slapping kind, but a quiet kind. I tell you, she could have had any man in this town. Why she even wanted to—'

Her voice tailed off, and she pushed the cigarette violently between her scarlet lips.

'Go on,' I urged. 'You were going to say something about her romance with Handford.'

The dark eyes reflected quick astonishment.

'You know about that?'

'Only a little,' I hedged. 'I'd be glad of anything else you cared to add.'

She flicked ash on the floor and I wondered how kindly Mrs. Andrews would react to that. Or maybe she'd become accustomed to it over the years.

'Did you come here for information that might help you find Jeannie Benson, or are you collecting pieces for a gossip column?'

I leaned forward in my chair to give emphasis to what I was going to say.

'Look, Francie, I'm asking you to believe that all I want is to find what happened to Miss Benson when she left Vale City. Now, I've been in this business a long time, and let me

100

tell you when you're looking for a missing person, no piece of information about that person can be discarded. And that includes gossip. So please, will you tell me about her and Handford?'

She listened carefully, watching my face as I spoke. I hoped the sincerity was squeezing out of every pore on my face. I was pushing it hard enough.

'O.K. Yes, I think I can see that,' she decided.

She'd stopped looking at my face and that was good. I didn't see how she could have missed the relief.

'Well, I was looking for a place on my own,' she began. 'I thought I wanted to be the independent business girl, you know? I've since realised all I really wanted was a break from the family. I love my family, but twenty years under the same roof is a long sentence for any group of people.'

I nodded to indicate I understood what she was driving at.

'I advertised in the *Clarion* for someone to room with me, and up came Jeannie Benson. She hadn't been in town long, she told me, and it would be a fine opportunity for her to get to know somebody who in turn knew their way around the town. I thought she seemed like a nice girl, and we made it a deal. It was fine for a few months. You know, living out of cans, and plenty of parties and so forth. Then Walt

Handford came into the picture.'

The change in her tone was noticeable but I made no comment.

'He took up more and more of her time. It was none of my business and I went my own way. I missed Jeannie's company naturally, but a girl has her own life to lead. I didn't realise how far things had gone before I got back here early one night. My date hadn't shown, and I thought I might as well catch an early night.'

She was looking troubled now, and suddenly switched the conversation.

'Are private investigators sort of like doctors and priests? I mean, do you have any kind of oath or something, that you mustn't repeat what you hear?'

I wagged my head sideways.

'Uh uh,' I negatived. 'No oath. But we do have our reputations to think of. I like to think mine is pretty good. No, there isn't any oath, but you could have my word on it, if that'll do. Don't tell me about it, if you don't want to.'

She considered for a few moments, then heaved her shoulders.

'What's the difference after all this time? I think I do sort of trust you, anyhow.'

I acknowledged the half-compliment by inclining my head.

'As I say, I got back to the apartment several hours earlier than expected. They were in bed. Jeannie and Walt Handford, right there in our own apartment. That was a hell of a surprise all around, I'm telling you. I didn't stay, after I saw them. Guess I practically ran out of there. I went to a late movie and didn't get home again till around one in the morning. It was one of the biggest shocks of my life. To you it probably doesn't sound anything out of the ordinary. Couple of girls living together like that, some fun and games on the side is to be expected. But not from her, not from Jeannie. She was lots of fun, and she had this deep, romantic streak inside her, but Jeannie was not cheap. Oh, I've had plenty of chances to watch her with men. She was a girl any man would go after, and I'd be kidding if I told you she didn't like it. She was very fond of male company. Many's the time I've watched some wolf go to work on her, men with hard reputations to uphold. And always I knew they were going to wind up with a couple of long clinches in the back seat of an automobile, and nothing else. She wasn't a tease, it wasn't that. It was just that she enjoyed the clinches, and that was as far as she was prepared to go. And the men always respected her for it. I never heard of one case where the man accused her of leading him on. They knew she was fun, but she wasn't cheap. She had a lot of principles. She was Jeannie. I guess I'm making an awful mess out of explaining this,' she added apologetically.

No, Francie, not a mess. Just a perfectly genuine outpouring of affection for a girl who

103

used to be Jeannie Benson. A girl, I was beginning to realise, I was unlucky to have missed.

'You're doing fine, Francie,' I encouraged. 'I can see where it must have been a blow to find—what you did find that night.'

Francie bobbed her head up and down.

'It certainly was. When I finally decided it was safe to go back there, Jeannie was waiting up for me. She wanted to talk to me about it. We stayed up till four in the morning. We seemed to take it in turns to cry, while the other one did the comforting. She told me all about it. Handford has a wife in a mental home, and according to him it's his fault she's in there. It was a long time ago—he's much older, you know—and there isn't any question of love any more. But he has this duty complex about it. Says he has to be there waiting for her if she's ever well enough to leave that place.'

It was evident from the hardening tone of her voice that Francie Andrews was not impressed with Walt Handford.

'From the way you speak, you seem to doubt his sincerity,' I suggested.

She tossed her head and the short black hair jogged.

'His sincerity isn't and wasn't any concern of mine. I was only interested in her position, in what he was doing to Jeannie Benson,' she asserted. 'She hadn't any family at all, and I guess I felt a kind of responsibility for her.

104

And don't get me wrong. I'm not suggesting she didn't know what time of day it was. I'm merely saying that for her this was the main event, and I didn't think she'd be able to handle it. Dammit, I already knew she couldn't.'

'You tried to get her to break with Handford?'

'Of course. But I was wasting my time and my breath. What made it so hard was, she felt bad about it herself. Knew it was wrong, but she loved the man. The real thing, you know. When a girl finds love like that, it's going to take more than a well-meaning room-mate to break it up.'

I looked round for an ashtray, found one on a small table near the window.

'So you decided you'd have to split up?' I prompted.

'Not right away. I wasn't going to give in as easily as that. We had another week together, a week of endless argument and persuasion. Then, yes, I did give up. I came back home and Jeannie got another place by herself.'

'You were still friends?'

'Certainly. In my own stubborn way, I still half-hoped I'd get her to see reason in the end. I'd have been better occupied trying to push an elephant up a mountain.'

'No,' I contradicted, half absent-mindedly. 'When you have to do what's right, you have to do it.'

Francie flashed me a grateful look for that.

'So, if I've followed you correctly, you saw her from time to time after that. Then the last occasion was a couple of days before she left town and you have no idea why she did that or where she went?'

'No. It was a complete surprise to me. More than that, because she'd told me to call over to her place that weekend and she'd have something to tell me. I was hoping against hope she'd be making an announcement about her and Handford.'

My interest quickened then.

'Did she say it would be about that?'

'No,' she admitted. 'Didn't actually say so, but what else could be so important it would have to wait until next time I saw her? Aside from Walt Handford, she didn't have a complicated life.'

'Will you tell me one thing, Francie? What have you got against Handford?'

'I told you,' she protested. 'I didn't like him breaking up Jeannie's life that way.'

'Yes, I know, you told me that. But there's some other reason too, isn't there? Something which is not connected with Jeannie Benson at all.'

'Do you charge a lot of money for your services?' she demanded.

One thing I'll say for Francie Andrews, she was the quickest conversation diverter I'd met in a long time.

'You could call it a lot. In fact, plenty of

people will tell you I'm as expensive as hell. Why?'

'Oh, I was just thinking, you're probably worth it. You don't miss an awful lot, do you?'

'I try not to. What didn't you like about Handford?'

'Persistent, too. Well, I suppose there's no harm in telling you. There's no third party present, so there's no slander. That right?'

'That's right,' I confirmed.

'I think he's crooked. Don't misunderstand me, I don't think he sleeps with a tommy-gun under his pillow. Not that kind of crooked. But I think he gets too many of the city contracts. You know, roads, city buildings and so forth. Handford isn't the only construction company in town, but he gets ninety per cent of the city business.'

'So do plenty of companies in plenty of towns,' I pointed out. 'That doesn't make them crooked. It's a matter of which one puts up the most competitive price.'

She nodded in agreement.

'I know it. I worked for one' of the companies once. It's common talk around them that their prices are often lower than Handford's. Yet he always lands the contract. Well, that's it. You asked me what I don't like. I don't like a crook.'

I rose to go.

'Thanks for all you've told me, Francie. I don't know whether I'll ever find Jeannie, but if I do I'm going to tell her where to come if she's in need of a friend.'

Her lip trembled.

'You're sort of nice. I wish you all the luck in the world. Will you tell me if you find her?'

'I'll tell you.'

I took a card from my pocket and gave it to her.

'If ever you hear anything of her, or remember something that may help, call me, will you?'

She nodded, without speaking. At the street door I turned to get a last look at her.

'And Francie, take a tip from a world-weary old private eye. Don't go around talking to anybody about Handford the way you talked to me. O.K. ?'

She nodded again, and I set off down the narrow strip of path between the white shell. At the gate I waved and she waved back. Then I climbed into the Chev and headed for home. There didn't seem to be a lot more I could get from Vale City at the moment. As I turned off at the pioneer memorial I was wondering if I'd ever need to come back here, whether Jeannie Benson was now going out of my life as she had already from the lives of those I'd been talking with. Jeannie Benson, I reflected, you got a raw deal. Sweet, lovely, decent Jeannie, always a pleasant memory here in Vale City. I braked for a red light and casually glanced at the pedestrians going about their business.

Maybe some of them had known her, maybe they were even thinking about her right this minute.

The signal changed and I eased forward into the main stream which would carry me away from Vale and Jeannie Benson. I was headed home now, home to Monkton City which had never heard of her. Which had heard though, of a dope-taking B-girl named Ruby Capone whose cheap and nasty little life had been snuffed out so easily a couple of nights ago.

It was time to find out more about Ruby.

CHAPTER SEVEN

My stomach mumbled angrily as I walked up to the Villa Marina. I'd skipped lunch, and it was four-thirty on a sweltering afternoon, no time of day to be eating.

Selecting a name at random I leaned on the buzzer and waited for the click as the lock on the front door was released. The smell in the entrance hall hadn't improved since my last visit, and I was glad my call didn't necessitate any lingering on that floor. Tramping upstairs, I made my way to room seven, started to push the bell then remembered it didn't work. I tapped lightly with the tips of my fingers. After two attempts a woman's voice spoke uncertainly from the other side of the door. 'Who is it?'

I kept my voice to as near an imitation as I could muster, and relied on the thickness of the door to muffle my words.

'Took,' I whispered urgently, 'open up.'

She hesitated, and I tapped again rapidly. It seemed to help her make up her mind. Suddenly she released the catch and flung open the door. My foot was already inside and my body was close behind as she recognised me and tried desperately to get the door shut again.

I pushed her away and closed the door behind me. Rose was evidently not expecting company. All she was wearing was a soiled pink nightdress which had been designed more for advertising than to keep her warm.

'What the hell do you want?' she snarled, backing away.

'I've come to help you, Rose,' I returned. 'And you look as if you need it.'

It was true. Rose looked a mess. Her hair was hanging all over the place and her eyes were puffy from crying and lack of sleep. Stale make-up made her face look like a death-mask and there were dirty streaks where the tears had run. At the right shoulder somebody had ripped the flimsy material, and two ugly blue welts were clearly visible.

'I don't need no help from you,' she whined. 'You get outta here.'

110

I tutted, and pointed to the weals.

'You need somebody, Rose. Somebody who should have been around when you collected those.'

Her hand crept up to probe tenderly at the bruises.

'No use relying on Took,' I assured her. 'You won't be seeing him any more.'

There had been fear on her face before, now it was tinged with despair.

'So you say,' she told me.

I nodded.

'So I say. So Vander say, too. Took left town. He's washed up.'

Doubtfully she pulled at her lower lip.

'You're crazy. He'll be back.'

I grinned knowingly.

'You hear what happened to him last night, honey? Somebody took his knife away and broke his arm. Vander said he was all through. Told him to blow town. Ask anybody.'

She tried to cling to what remained of her confidence.

'Like who, for instance?'

'Like Ben. Ask Ben if you want. Or Jammy.'

At the mention of the little guy who lived in a private rainbow Rose reacted sharply. She pulled her head suddenly away as if in fear, and her lips curled back over her teeth in a snarl of hatred.

'So it was Jammy,' I said softly. 'Why'd he do that to you?' She shook her head dumbly, bit her lip, then burst into gales of tears. The deep sobs shook her whole body and she abandoned herself to the outburst, ignoring me completely. I reflected it would probably be best to leave her to cry it out. Parking in a chair, I waited. The fit seemed to go on for hours, but my watch insisted it was only a couple of minutes. Gradually she pulled herself together, the sobs became less frequent.

'You—you gotta cigarette?' she asked brokenly.

I took her the pack and held the lighter steady while her twitching fingers attempted to steady the end of the tube in the flame. Finally she made it, inhaled deeply and sighed.

'That's good. I haven't had one all day.'

'There's a kiosk just across the street,' I reminded her.

She made no reply but went and dumped herself in a chair. She didn't sit down, or settle herself. She literally dumped herself down, squatting inelegantly where she landed staring moodily at the lighted smoke.

At first she didn't answer. She was so preoccupied I wasn't even certain she'd heard. I repeated the question. This time I got some response. She shuddered, shook herself as if to free herself of some unpleasant thought, and looked at me vaguely.

'You say something?'

I put the question for the third time. Still I

didn't get an answer. Instead she said:

'That's on the level, what you said about Took, isn't it? He's run off and left me here.'

It wasn't a question. It was a statement of fact, delivered in a flat lifeless voice.

'You won't be seeing him again. I should have thought you'd be glad.'

She snorted derisively.

'Glad? Yeah, I can see where you would think that. What do you know about people like us, Took and me. We don't live in the same world.'

'I could probably make a fair guess,' I replied. 'Girl like you can get in a lot of trouble in a town like this if she's all alone. So somebody like Took happens. He's mean and he's nasty and he takes every red cent you make. He gives you nothing but trouble, but he's all the trouble you get. His side is to make sure nobody else tries to push you around. You hate him and you wish him dead a dozen times a week, but you know he's your protection. Without him you're open season for every weirdo, every pimp and hoodlum in town. Right?'

Without interest she said:

'I guess it'll do.'

'How did you come to let Jammy in here? You must have been expecting Took, weren't you?'

She hesitated, then shrugged.

'Ah, what's the difference? I may as well tell

113

you. I know Took's gone, I was certain of it last night. Just I've been kidding myself all day maybe he'd come back. Just as well I did, too. I'd have gone crazy else. Well, this is the bottom of the slide for me, brother. Nothing lower can happen to me now. What do you want to know?'

'First tell me what happened here,' I suggested.

'Oh, that. Well it was getting kinda late at the joint last night. Took hadn't showed up, and I was getting worried about him. Well, not about him, really. More about what might happen to me if he didn't show. That's a pretty rugged end of town at two in the morning, especially for a dame like me who doesn't have a lot of clothes on in the first place. Then this Jammy'—she shuddered—'He comes up to me and says Took's been on the phone. He can't make it to the club, and he's promised Jammy ten bucks if he makes sure I get back here all right. I wasn't sure about it at first, but that Jammy he's pretty smart. Know how he sold me?'

I shook my head.

'He said he couldn't live on promises. He had expenses. He'd only bring me home if I paid the money in advance. Well, that convinced me. That's the kind of language I can understand. So I gave him the two fives and he says O.K. Then he has this car outside and we come here.'

114

Her voice was less confident as she reached the part of the story which connected with the bruises on her shoulder.

'I thought he'd leave me downstairs, but he says no. The deal with Took was that Jammy had to check up here, make sure I hadn't got some guy waiting for me. If there was anybody he was to tell Took. And I knew what would happen then.'

'You believed that, too?' I queried.

Rose shrugged.

'You don't know much about guys like Took. If he made a deal that's exactly the kind of thing he'd think of. And that I would expect him to think of. Jammy knew that, and we came up. He—he started the minute we got inside. He had a sap with him, you know those things, they're like solid rubber with a thong one end?'

I nodded grimly.

'I've seen them.'

'Well, the minute we got inside he hit me with this thing. That's where I got these,' she pointed to the damaged shoulder.

'That was just the warm-up. He really laid into me, I thought he was going to kill me, but he's too smart for that. He didn't even knock me unconscious, just kept on soaking into me, here—and here—and—all over. Then he— he—say how about another cigarette?'

She cut off her story and I moved fast with the Old Favourites before she broke down

115

again. She dragged deeply at the smoke, rubbed a hand over her face, and continued.

'Well, afterwards he was like a crazy man, you know? Tell you the truth, I thought maybe he was crazy, because I knew what Took would do when he found out about all this. Then this thing, Jammy, he told me about Took. Told me he'd left town and he'd never dare to come back. Jammy was moving in, and the little work-out we'd just had, was to let me know what would happen to me if he ever caught me holding out, or trying to double-cross him. I didn't believe him at first, didn't want to believe him. But all the time I was afraid it could be true. And what made me think so was the way Jammy was carrying on. I knew he didn't have the guts to do what he'd done to Took's woman, if there was any chance of Took finding out. Only I wasn't Took's woman any more. I belonged to Jammy and that was the lowest moment of my whole life. I knew there was nothing I could do about it, I never felt so—so—desperate. That's it. I don't know how long all this went on, maybe a coupla hours. Finally he took every cent I'd got, belted me another twice so I'd remember, and told me to stay right here till he came back for me tonight.'

'And you've been here all day?'

'You wouldn't have to ask that if you'd seen what he did to me last night.'

It wasn't a pretty story, but it wasn't unusual

116

for a girl like Rose. What these girls won't realise is that they can never win.

'What're you going to do now?' I asked.

'I've had all day to think about that,' she responded slowly. 'This is the end of the line for little Rose Schwartz. I've been places and done things people wouldn't dream. But Jammy is as far as I go. I'm going to kill him.'

If she'd screamed it, I'd have said it was hysteria. If she'd spat it out I'd have said histrionics. But her tone was normal, almost conversational. What I'd just heard was nothing but the literal truth. Rose was going to eliminate Jammy.

'Do you need to, Rose?'

'Huh? I don't get it.'

'I mean, you want Jammy dead, O.K. But do you have to do it yourself? Are you sure you couldn't tell me anything that would put Jammy in the death-chamber. I'm talking about Ruby and Lola. Did Jammy have anything to do with their deaths?'

She looked at me dispassionately.

'I don't know. Ask him.'

'I'm asking you.'

'I don't know, I tell you. Listen, if I could get the law to rub out that little bastard for me, you think I wouldn't do it?'

'I don't know, Rose. You have some awful funny rules, you people. It's all right for you to do something to somebody, but you mustn't talk to the law about them.'

She laughed shortly.

'You're kidding yourself if you think that jazz means a thing to me. Even if it did, Jammy is outside of any rules. Anyway what's that about talking to the law? That what you are, a lawman? Not that it bothers me. I'm still going to kill him.'

'No, I'm not the law. I'm private. But I am interested in what happened to Ruby Capone. Are you going to help me?'

'How can I help you?' she queried. 'I don't know anything. I went next door to talk to Ruby, she was dead. That's all there is. If it's any help to you, you can have it. But that's all there is.'

'What time was it, Rose?' I asked.

'Oh, let's see, I did tell the cops all this, you know. I think it was around three-thirty, three forty-five. 'Bout that.'

'And you just happened to go see her at that hour?'

'This is breaking a regulation or something? We were kind of friends. I went to see her. Where's the harm?'

'No harm, Rose. Did you often call next door at that time of the morning?'

'I couldn't sleep and I went to borrow cigarettes.'

She came out with that line pat. Much too pat. It was like an automatic vending machine. You pushed the button marked 'reason for visit' and out came the metallic voice 'to borrow cigarettes'.

'That's the same story you told the police, isn't it?'

'Why wouldn't it be? This is what happened. Why would I tell those guys anything different?'

'Why?'

Slowly, almost absent-mindedly, I drew the billfold from my inside pocket. It was thickly populated with green folding money. Casually I peeled off two twenties and a ten and dropped them on the table.

'What were we saying, Rose? Oh, yes. Why should you tell the police anything different? I'll tell you why. Because it was two days ago. And two days ago things *were* different. Two days ago you had all kinds of things to think about. Like Took for instance. You naturally wouldn't want to do anything that might get Took in dutch. But now it isn't like that. Now there isn't any Took. He's blown town and left you to look after yourself. Left you to Jammy. And now you have to look out for Rose Schwartz. And this,' I tapped at the bills, 'this could be anything you wanted. A gun for Jammy. A railroad ticket out of Monkton. Anything you wanted. What do you say, Rose?'

The bills seemed to hypnotise her. Money is an odd commodity. To different people it can mean different things. To Rose Schwartz at that moment, fifty dollars meant the margin between despair and some kind of hope.

'I—I don't know whether I can help you,' she whispered.

'You can help me,' I asserted positively. 'Start by telling me about Ruby Capone.'

'What about her?'

'It's my fifty, baby. I ask the questions. How long did you know her?'

She stared at the floor.

'A few weeks, maybe months. Time don't mean a thing in my life.'

'All right. How'd you come to meet her?'

'At the joint. She walked in one night, and just kind of stayed.'

I lit an Old Favourite. It was evident from the lifelessness of Rose's replies, that she either didn't know much, or else was guarding her tongue with more than average care. With people like Jammy for playmates I knew the fix she was in. You don't get a new body for fifty dollars.

'She get in any trouble with Vander?' I asked suddenly.

Rose looked surprised.

'Trouble? They were playing footsie a coupla days after she arrived. That was a funny thing, though.'

'Funny? What way, funny?'

She heaved her shoulders, then winced and nursed her bruises.

'Mr. Vander—and he's always mister—' she emphasised, 'he always swore he'd have nothing to do with the girls around the club. Mr. Vander has a very low opinion of us. We're not good enough for him.'

'I see. But he didn't feel that way about Ruby?'

'No. I couldn't see the difference, not then, not right away. Ruby looked like the rest of us, dressed the same way, even tried to talk the language.'

I noticed a hesitation.

'Tried to. You mean she didn't sound natural?'

Rose finally displayed sufficient animation to look irritable.

'What do you want, you want I should spell it out for you? Well O.K., all right. The girls at the Peek-a-Boo Club, me and the rest, are a bunch of tramps. That's what we are, and we're not complaining. This Ruby, she never really made the team.'

That might have been plain enough spelling for Rose but I pressed for more details.

'But you said she looked like the rest,' I probed.

'Sure. Like dressing up for Christmas, you know? I always figured Ruby for a phoney. She'd stand around down there like any five-dollar whore, then she'd go and louse it up some way. Some of those guys can get kinda free with their hands. Ruby didn't try to stop 'em or anything silly like that. Just she used to look like she wasn't used to it, you know? And

121

we could never figure where she came from, either. We've all been around a little bit, made the scene in like maybe Vegas, Frisco, L.A., even Mexico City. One of the girls came right here from Miami.'

There was a hint of boastfulness here. I was to gather that only the high-priced broads worked Miami.

'What's this to do with Ruby?'

'Like I'm saying,' she continued witheringly, 'we been around. You can usually find some place you both been to, some name you both knew. Wasn't like that with Ruby. Like she dropped out of the sky.'

'Could have been she was wanted by the police somewhere. Keeping your mouth shut can be awful handy if you want to stay out of jail,' I suggested.

Rose nodded in agreement.

'That's what we finally figured. She wasn't cut out for our business, not really. Little things she did, or didn't do. You can always tell. So we figured finally it was like you say. She was just a chump dame who did something, maybe pushed her boy-friend off a roof or something, and now she was like learning a new trade.'

'So Mr. Vander thought he'd make an exception in Ruby's case, huh?'

'Yeah. He really seemed to go for her. Funny thing, not that I was jealous or like that, but I would have thought she was kind of scrawny for an important guy like that.'

She looked down at herself, and passed a hand thoughtfully over one of her heavy breasts. Rose couldn't see how anybody could pass up what she had to offer in favour of the scrawny Ruby.

'But he still let her go on working the place?' I queried.

'Yeah, but hustling drinks only. No rough stuff with the clientele. If any of 'em got out of line, wanted to know when he got some value for all the money he was spending, Ben or the wrestler would heave him out on his can.'

'The wrestler?'

'The bar-jockey,' she explained. 'They call him that, on account he was a pro one time.'

'Oh. So Ruby was Vander's personal property, really?'

'Really was,' nodded Rose.

'Then how come he let her go on pumping herself full of happy juice?' I queried.

'I don't know nothing about that,' she informed me. 'But it's kind of a wacky question, ain't it?'

'What way?'

'Every which way. You get somebody, a dame or any other somebody, they're on the stuff. You don't just tell 'em to lay off. Not even if you're Vander. If they're on it, they're on it. Period.'

'Where did Ruby get her supplies?'

'Look, that money on the table, that's fifty

bucks, right?'

'Right.'

'So ask me do I need the fifty, all right I need it. I want to get outta this town. Because Vander run Took out, and let Jammy loose on me. I'll tell you about Vander. Ruby's dead, so all right I'll tell you about her too. But don't ask me about those guys, the ones who handle the merchandise. There ain't so much money in the world it'll hide me from the big operators if I put the finger on 'em. Ask me about Vander.'

That made too much sense for me to attempt to argue Rose out of it. The happy dust corporation had branches everywhere, and when you have a multi-million dollar business, you don't permit the Rose Schwartzes of this world to put it in jeopardy. But I didn't ask her about Vander. Instead I said:

'And Lola Wade? How about her?'

'Lola? Suddenly we're talking about Lola?'

'I like to move the conversation around. You know, keep it lively. What about Lola? Was she one of the regular girls, or was she like Ruby too?'

The ghost of a smile flitted across the chewed lipstick.

'Lola? Ah, brother, she wasn't nobody's Ruby. Not that one. Lola knew every cathouse in the state. Lola had been around, you bet.'

'How long did you know her?'

'Coupla months. Came down from Fresno. That Lola, she knew everybody and everything. She was a load of laughs.'

'Why was she killed?'

Rose looked shocked.

'You ask me that? Listen, I don't know nothing about that. In our line of business you meet all kinds of creeps. If you're real unlucky you get a real gone weirdo. Guess that's what happened to Lola.'

I had no doubt Rose was telling what she considered to be the plain truth. There was no attempt at hedging here. But it was also significant that it hadn't even occurred to Rose that Lola might not have been murdered at all, but could have died either by accident, through taking an overdose of heroin, or by her own hand, deliberately.

'Funny though, her dying the same way Ruby died,' I suggested.

'Funny? Oh sure, a real ball. I near bust a rib laughing over it,' she informed me bitingly.

'You know I don't mean it that way,' I corrected. 'What I meant was it was a hell of a coincidence. First Ruby, then Lola, both with the same consignment of H. You don't suppose Lola could just have made a mistake, the way Ruby did?'

'A mistake? Lola? You're kidding. Lola told me herself she'd been juicing it up for more than a year. She was real gone. People like that they don't make mistakes with the merchandise. They know the smell of it and the feel of it better'n half the regular druggists. When you're paying that kind of money for something you have to know what you're buying.'

'And Lola had a big habit, huh?'

'Big,' she nodded. 'She was one of the best customers in the neighbourhood, so I heard.'

There was a lot of sense in what Rose was saying. There was so much adulteration of dope these days, that the people who were heavy addicts quickly became expert at assessing the strength of the supply they were buying. If Lola Wade had been as habitual with her dosage as Rose suggested, it was improbable that she would make a fatal mistake like that. Not impossible of course, nothing is. But it was a long shot I couldn't count when assessing the field.

'Where did you hear this, about Lola being such a good customer?'

Rose's face went blank and she began picking at a loose thread on a cushion.

'Something about Vander you wanted to know?' she asked.

I wasn't going to catch her on anything involving the dope traffic. And, aside from that, I didn't feel Rose Schwartz had much more to tell me.

'Go pack a bag,' I instructed. 'I've got a car outside. I'll take you to the station, see you right on to the train.'

She was undecided.

'Just like that?' she queried. 'It's kind of sudden.'

'Last night Jammy was kind of sudden,' I reminded her. 'And tonight you'll see him again if you stick around.'

That helped to make up her mind.

'Guess you're right,' she said wearily. 'I won't take long.'

Fifteen minutes later she was dressed for the street, and her stuff was inside a grey crocodile grip. She was still dazed by the sudden turn of events which had led up to this sudden departure from town, and was quite docile about everything I told her to do. As we were about to leave the apartment she said nervously:

'Hey, there's something I'd like you to have.'

'Oh?'

'Yeah.' She shifted from one foot to the other, like a kid caught out raiding the apple store. 'Here, this is it.'

She thrust out her hand with a photograph in it. Taken in daylight, it showed a man and a girl standing beside a station wagon laughing at the photographer. In the background was the pioneer memorial in Vale City. The man was Walter F. Handford, and the girl's face was familiar. The only picture I'd ever seen of Ruby Capone was the mask-like newspaper reproduction taken after death. This girl had a strange resemblance to Ruby, except that she was from another world. A vibrant, warm-looking creature, with a smiling confidence far removed from the brassy assurance of Ruby. This, I knew, was Jeannie Benson.

'Where'd you get this, Rose?' I asked.

She looked almost shame-faced.

'Well, it was after we found her, you know? Once I got over the shock and all, I figured I might as well look round. If there was anything in the place I had as much right to it as some sticky-fingered cop. Ruby didn't have nobody to leave anything to.'

It was too late in life for me to try educating Rose into different ways of thinking. From her point of view, what she'd done had every justification. I said:

'Was this all?'

'No. There was some money, about eighty dollars I think. I didn't touch nothing else, just this picture here. I kind of liked Ruby, it didn't seem like no harm.'

'Why are you giving it to me?'

'You're so interested in her, and all, I figured you might like it. I don't need a thing to remind me of this town.'

I nodded, studied the picture again, slipped it in my pocket.

'Rose, you told the police and everybody else that you found Ruby's body yourself.'

'Sure,' she confirmed vigorously, 'that's how it was.'

'No, it wasn't, baby,' I said in a hard voice. 'Just now you said, "after we found her". "We" Rose. That means like two or more people. Who was with you? Or shall we just forget the whole thing and I'll call up Jammy and tell him you're waiting for him?'

She shuddered.

'All right. It can't make no difference now, I guess. Took and me, we were together. It was him had the money and stuff from Ruby's apartment. He'd have even had that picture too I bet, if I hadn't stuck it in my purse.'

'I can imagine. How did you come to call on her at that hour?'

'That was the bit I couldn't tell the cops, and why Took had to stay outta sight. He told me she'd left word at the club she wanted him to bring her some merchandise. You know, in the little white packets. That's why we went in there. Now ask me why I didn't tell the law all that.'

I could certainly understand why not, but there was another thing I did want to ask.

'Rose, you have told me all along you wouldn't talk to me about the dope peddling. Now suddenly you come out with a thing like this. Why?'

My voice was loaded with suspicion, but all it produced was a look of mild surprise.

'I'm not changing the tune,' she told me. 'Took had nothing to do with those guys. It was just he was to bring the packet for Ruby.

129

Somebody at the club gave it to him. Just a favour, nothing else.'

'I see.'

There was nothing else for us to talk about either. I drove her to Central and watched her aboard the local to L.A. On a last-minute impulse I gave her another twenty dollars. It was a crazy thing to do and I knew it. There'd be somebody like Took waiting around in L.A. to take away any cash carried by somebody like Rose Schwartz.

She clutched the bills and said throatily,

'You're a funny guy. What's all this to you anyway?'

'Nothing,' I assured her. 'I'm just a nut who likes to watch girls go out on trains.'

Then the whistle blew, and Rose was shunting slowly away from Monkton City to new surroundings. New surroundings? I doubted that. Another town maybe, but that's where the difference would end. Within a few days at most, Rose would be back at the same old stand. Another rathole like the Peek-a-Boo Club. Another Took. When you're Rose Schwartz what else can you do?

I walked out the front of the station. Two men came towards me. They wore expensive crease-free summer suits and beautiful cream silk shirts. They could have been advertising men, or studio front-office men or what-have-you. But in my business you have to learn to distinguish between one kind of people and another. And I knew these two, although their faces were not familiar. They were the mob.

'Boss wants you,' greeted the shorter man.

'That's nice,' I smiled. 'And who might the boss be?'

'Mr. Benito, he's the boss,' returned the short man, pleasantly. 'Do you have to hear any more?'

'No,' I admitted. 'Where do we go?'

'We'll get along,' acknowledged the other. 'You drive your own car. I'll come with you. Like for company.'

I climbed into the Chev and the talker got in next to me. The other man moved towards a cream Cadillac that was parked a few spaces behind me.

'Where to?' I asked my new friend.

'Just follow him,' he told me. 'And, so there's no misunderstanding drive careful.'

From his pocket he removed a long-barrelled .22 revolver and rested it negligently on his knees.

The .22 is the weapon only of the expert shot, the bigtime pro enforcer.

I drove carefully.

CHAPTER EIGHT

The Caddy swung out of traffic and pulled up. I squeezed in behind and sat right where I was.

131

Buddy-boy with the .22 hadn't said anything about me getting out, and I didn't want to be the cause of any little misunderstandings. Especially one which might wind up with me wearing a hole somewhere.

The man next to me smiled. He had a pleasant smile and a nice row of strong white teeth. To me he smelled of death. I hated his insides.

'He said you were smart. Boss always knows. O.K. feller, out.'

The other man was already standing on the sidewalk, waiting. I got out. We were standing outside an Italian restaurant which I knew was a front for a bookie joint. With my new friends ranged either side of me I went into the place. A little grey-haired man in an apron looked us over with interest then jerked his head towards the rear and nodded. There were only two customers and both were dawdling over coffee cups from which there was no steam. They were as much part of the furniture as the chairs and dirty tables. We carried on through a door at the back and into a large room where a number of men in shirtsleeves were busy working at black ledgers. Business was through for the day, and these were the results-men, the boys who could add up a whole page of figures at a glance. I've seen them work before, and they are the best in the add-up business.

'Wait,' said the taller of my escorts.

I perched my rear against a vacant table. It was evident from the attitude of those who'd come to collect me that they hadn't any hostile intentions. They'd been told to bring me here and that was all. I didn't waste any time speculating about what Benito wanted. When he was ready, he'd tell me. Instead I asked one of the serious-faced bookworms a question.

'How'd we make out today?'

He looked up at me with a pained expression.

'Jokes? At this hour I gotta listen to jokes? You want to know how we make out today, any day, you ask the boss. Don't ask me, Mister. I'm just a computer that talks.'

'Knock it off,' growled the man beside me.

The other accountant blanched and turned his head quickly back to his books. After a while the tall one came back.

'Boss'll see you now,' he told me. 'In there and the first door you come to.'

Nobody seemed to be coming with me so I made the ten-yard journey all by myself. I found the door, knocked and opened it. Rudy Benito was sitting in a big leather chair facing the door.

'You want to see me?' I queried.

'That's why you're here,' he grunted. 'Shut the door and sit down.'

There was no one else in the room. I closed the door firmly and sat on the only other chair, a rickety wooden affair.

'Thought you went back up to the Bay,' I told him.

'Nobody asked you what you thought.' He seemed to say it almost absent-mindedly, as though his thoughts were on other things.

'You were supposed to call me, tell me how you were doing.'

'All those numbers were San Francisco numbers. If you haven't been there what makes you think I didn't call?' I countered.

'You didn't call,' he repeated flatly. 'If you'd of called I'd know it.'

'There's been nothing to tell,' I assured him.

'So tell me the nothing,' he insisted.

I gave him a few details of what I'd been doing. Not too many, and for a very good reason. I'd listened with care to what he'd told me the day before and one thing I knew that the rest of the world didn't. Benito had some traces of human feeling left in him. It was true they were all concentrated, too concentrated, on his daughter. But they were there just the same. To the rest of the world, Benito was little more than a machine. A powerful money-making machine, and it was precisely that coldness that took him up to the high mob-ranks. Machines don't make mistakes, don't get emotional. In the hierarchy of the organisation these are prime virtues. But I knew that where Jeannie Benson was concerned, this man had some almost-ordinary feelings. That was bad. People with feelings

134

make mistakes, get worked up about things. And that was why I was being careful not to tell Benito too much. He might jump to conclusions, just like any ordinary man might do. But he wasn't any ordinary man, he was Benito. And when he decided to do a thing, he could get it done quick. If I told him too much, any one of the people I'd talked to in the past twenty-four hours might find themselves on the next refrigerated slab to Ruby Capone before the night was out.

I told him enough to make it sound like sense, and no more.

'You done all right,' he said grudgingly. 'Not good, but all right. What about this Handford. What do you think?'

'Too early for me to think anything,' I replied carefully. 'He seems O.K.'

'Seems ain't enough. Now, you get after him. I'm not asking whether he seems O.K. What I want to know, is he O.K. or not? Get after him.'

'All right. I was going to check him out anyway.'

'Do that. What's the King Arthur bit?'

'Huh?'

'You heard me. This tramp, this Schwartz. What's with tossing my dough around that way, and helping her get outta town?'

I'd known he wouldn't be able to understand that one.

'I don't like the look of this guy Jammy,

135

works for Vander,' I said carefully. 'Figured if I upset him a little bit, like taking Rose away from him, he might do something.'

'What kind of something?' enquired Benito craftily.

'Something foolish, I hope. I'm not saying he knows anything about what happened to Ruby, maybe he doesn't. But he certainly knows something, this way I might find out what it is. If he gets mad enough at me he might try to do something about it.'

Benito considered this, then shook his head slowly.

'No catch. If this Jammy knows something, why not just take him down some alley and beat his brains out till he tells you what it is?'

It was my turn to shake my head.

'For one thing I'm not that certain. For another, if Jammy is in touch with the big-leaguers he'll be more scared of them than he is of me. You should know that.'

He acknowledged this with a brief grin.

'Still no catch. If you're not going to get anything out of the guy, why go to all that trouble?'

Patiently I said:

'I didn't mean I think he'll talk at all. What I'm trying to say is, he may lead me somewhere. People who get mad don't think straight. He could just charge off somewhere and put me on to somebody I don't even know about yet. Like I said, it's all long shots in this business. You annoy a few people, maybe one of 'em does something foolish.'

'I get it,' he agreed doubtfully. 'That's why you trod on Vander's corns, huh?'

'Right,' I acknowledged. 'You satisfied now, or do you want me off this hunt?'

'Off?' he was puzzled. 'Why would I want you off?'

'You don't seem to have a lot of faith in me, sending those two mugs to pick me up twenty-four hours after I started work.'

It was a calculated risk on my part to put on the wounded act. Benito looked surprised.

'What do you want? Yesterday I give you five grand in cash money. In my business a man learns to be careful. Guy who don't watch out for his investments is practically dead. It's just a friendly talk, ain't it?'

'When I want to talk to my friends, I call 'em on the phone, or else I go see them. I don't send armed gorillas out to snatch 'em off the street.'

He chuckled.

'Sure you don't, but who are you? Me, I'm Benito. I do what I want. Anyway,' he shrugged, 'it's just habit, I guess. What're you beefing about? For five grand you should have such tender feelings. Keep in touch, huh?'

The interview seemed to be over. I got up from my unstable perch and said:

'How do I do that? You still want me to call San Francisco or is there somewhere round here I can reach you?'

'Beats me how you keep out of trouble,' he sighed. 'Nobody ever asks me where I'm going. Use the numbers I already gave you.'

'Kay.'

I went out and back to the main room. The two goons who'd brought me to the party were standing together talking. They didn't even look round as I came out from seeing the big man. I walked up to them and tapped one on the shoulder, the one who'd ridden beside me in the car.

'Benito's through with me now,' I informed him.

'So,' he shrugged. 'So blow.'

'How d'you know it's O.K. for me to leave?' I queried. The other man said:

'It's O.K., Preston. The boss just wanted to talk with you. There wasn't supposed to be any trouble.'

I didn't look at him. To my ex-passenger I said:

'I'm not talking to him, I'm talking to you.'

He seemed slightly surprised, but not angry. Yet.

'You heard him, just the same. Now will you beat it?'

'Not for a minute,' I told him. 'You knew all Benito wanted was talk, didn't you?'

'So?'

'So I don't like people waving guns at me. Especially pigs in three-hundred dollar suits.'

He spoke very quietly then, but there was a sudden whiteness at his lips and throat. His eyes were slits and I knew this was a very dangerous man. But I was already mad enough not to care about that.

'Did you say pig, Chump?'

'Pig,' I repeated. 'I don't like pigs who shove guns in my face. I'm afraid of guns. They kill people.'

There was a stillness in the room. No longer was anybody making any pretence of checking the books. They were watching anxiously, waiting to see if they'd need to move out of the way in a hurry. The man facing me was no longer casual and relaxed. He was tense all over. Tension seemed to vibrate from him.

'So they do, they do kill people,' he agreed. 'If you got any brains, people, you'll get outta here kinda sudden. The boss don't like any trouble in here.'

'Isn't going to be any,' I assured him, moving one pace backwards as if to leave. With this guy I'd have to leave the rules at home. I kicked him hard in the kneecap. He doubled slightly with the sudden pain. As he did I brought my locked fists up into his face. Something squelched, and a roar of agonised fury came from him as his head was knocked back. Immediately I sliced him across the throat with the side of my palm. He took a wild swing at me which landed just over the heart. It jolted me but there was no time for

139

catching breath. Moving in close I hit him twice low in the belly, and as he automatically hunched I butted him in the face with the top of my head. He threw both hands up to his ruined face and screamed with pain. I punched him hard in the throat and he was all through for the day. As he went down, I punched him on the back of the neck for good measure.

The redness was all out of my head now as I stood over him, breathing heavily. The other man, the Cadillac driver, hadn't moved since it started.

'You got a nasty temper there,' he informed me easily. 'Could get you in trouble.'

'You going to make some?' I queried.

He shrugged nonchalantly.

'This is nothing to do with me. This is you and him. He ain't gonna like you when he wakes up.'

'Too bad. I know him, guys like him. Makes him feel like a real big hero to make people jump around when he shows the iron. You think he lost this argument? He won it before it started. All he's got is maybe a few lumps. In a week they'll be gone. I lost a year off my life in that car.'

He didn't get it, and I wasn't going to waste any time explaining it to him. Guns are so familiar to everybody these days, they think it hardly counts if somebody merely points one at somebody else and doesn't shoot it off. That's not the way I feel about it. In my

140

business a gun is a thing that kills people. It's not something you carry for kicks, or to point at people if you don't mean to use it. The kind of company I keep, anybody steers an iron in my direction it means the chances are at least even they're thinking of squeezing the trigger. It's bad enough in the ordinary line of work. To have some clown point one at me with no intention and for no reason except it makes him feel important, that gets to me fast.

I was still breathing noisily when I climbed into the Chev and drove away.

CHAPTER NINE

It was a few minutes after eight that night when I walked into Sam's. Sam's is just a bar, like any one of the other sixty-one bars in Monkton City, but nobody else made such a fuss of me. In some ways I'm human, and although I always tell Sam to knock it off, it's funny how I keep turning up in the place.

Business was fifty-fifty, especially the vast blonde who was spread untidily all over one end of the counter. She was fifty on both counts, around the chest and date of birth. Sam jerked his head to warn me to sit further along. The warning was appreciated but unnecessary. I was a long way off being that desperate.

'Hi, Sam.'

I settled at the far end from the mountain of flesh.

'What'll it be, Mr. Preston?'

'My shirt buttons have been banging on my spine most of the day,' I told him. 'What could that be, Sam?'

He smiled with joy.

'Nothing to stop 'em, Mr. Preston. You have an empty stummick. And I'm glad to hear it.'

I looked pained.

'Sam, I don't like to hear you talk that way. You're glad because I can't afford regular meals?'

He threw up his hands.

'Please, Mr. Preston. Don't make me bleed all over the bar. If you gotta empty stummick, it's because you been too busy with some broad to stop for anything. I meant something else.'

With Sam I've got the life. We both live in the same town, but our worlds are different. Sam's world is a small house with too many kids, too little money, a five-year-old car. The rest of his life is filled with overflowing ashtrays and booze-bums. My world is full of fast shiny cars, broads in black silk pyjamas waiting in every top-price block of apartments for me to call. Millionaires, movie-stars, always a little respectful when I'm around, confident that I won't reveal The Secret to the world outside. That's what Sam thinks. I was

142

tempted to tell him about the enforcer with the long-barrelled .22, but I couldn't spoil his fun like that. Instead I asked the expected question.

'What did you mean, Sam?'

His eyes shone with pleased anticipation.

'I meant I have in the kitchen the biggest, the bestest pork chop you ever laid eyes on. I been saving it up all day, hoping one of my real special customers would look in.'

Good old Sam.

'I'm your boy,' I told him. 'I'll take a beer while I'm waiting.'

I carried the glass over to a side booth and sat down. I didn't want to sit at the bar and have a chin fest with Sam. What I wanted was to think, and the empty booth seemed built for the purpose. Lighting an Old Favourite, I leaned back and took stock of how far I'd got. It wasn't far.

A girl named Gina Benito ran out on her hoodlum father and became Jeannie Benson. Jeannie lived in a small town and seemed to be headed for a normal life. She met a man named Walter Handford, and that appeared to have been a turning point. Handford had an invalid wife. Jeannie stuck it as long as she could, then one day got a good square look at herself and moved on. So far it was fine. It made sense. If what I'd heard about her was anywhere near the truth, she sounded like the kind of girl who'd have enough backbone to pull herself out of a mess like that, go off somewhere else and start again. Only she didn't. This was the part that made no sense to me. All she had to do was get another job and start picking up the pieces of her life. But she didn't. She went straight downhill as fast as she could travel, became a drink-promoter, and who knows what else, for a cheap crook named Vander, in a third-rate joint on Conquest Street. With me it didn't sit right. If there'd been a quarrel with Handford, that might have upset her emotionally, maybe enough to send her bad for a few days. Even a week. It's a curious fact that the reactions of women who have a busted romance are as diverse as the sand-patterns on a seashore. It is also well-known that the more conventional their life has been up to that point, the more drastic their reactions seem to be. Understand when I say women, I'm talking only of real women, not the prissy, milk-and-water variety. So it was not so much what Jeannie had done that surprised me, it was the length of time it lasted. Days, even a few weeks I could have stomached. But six months of that kind of living did not jell with my picture of Jeannie Benson.

That was the first thing I couldn't understand. There was the big query mark of how and why she died. Not to mention where. According to Rourke, she'd been taken to the Villa Marina after she died, and if Rourke said so that was how it happened. But I put the death question on one side for a while. All the other questions had to be answered before I could tackle that one. For example, there was Took. I didn't think Rose Schwartz had been holding out on me that afternoon. I thought she'd told me what she knew about Jeannie's death. Took was to take some dope to Jeannie's—or rather Ruby's apartment that night. But why? The girl wasn't in need of supplies, couldn't have been, considering she'd died a few hours earlier of an over-dose. So either Took knew she was dead, and wanted the body found, or else whoever sent him there knew what he was going to find. I liked that better. It would be a kind of shield, to indicate there was no foreknowledge that she was dead. A killer likes the body to remain undiscovered for as long as possible, in the ordinary way. It makes everybody's job that much tougher. Fixing the exact time of death for example, getting accurate stories from everyone about their movements, who they saw, and so forth. By sending Took to the apartment, a specially-clever killer could be protecting himself in an involved, round about way. Obviously he could not know the girl was dead, otherwise he would try to avoid establishing any connection that night between her and himself. But why Took? He wasn't exactly what the police would welcome as a God-fearing upright citizen kind of witness.

That line of enquiry wasn't getting me anywhere at all. Anyway I needed another beer. Walking across to Sam I had the glass recharged, then wandered back to the booth and my thoughts. They weren't encouraging.

There was Lola Wade. It seemed fairly certain she'd been murdered. It may have no connection with the death of Gina Jeannie Ruby Benito Benson Capone, but I would have hated to count on it. Why then had Lola died, and assuming a connection with Ruby, what was it? Well, at least that was one positive piece of action I could take. Lola had last been in Fresno. If there was anything about her up there that might indicate a link with Ruby, I could at least start to find out.

Too, I wasn't satisfied with Walter F. Handford. He seemed all right, but for all I knew he could be the top man representing the mob in Vale City. That could be an explanation. It could have been Handford who first induced Jeannie Benson to start taking drugs, so he could set her up for the short trip to Monkton City, and a new life as B-girl Ruby Capone. The gag about the stolen car didn't fool me either. Obviously Ruby had been murdered by Handford. Then he dumped her in the car, drove over to Monkton and got her back into her own apartment. After that he got rid of the car and reported it stolen from outside City Hall in Vale. Then he blackmailed the other twelve—or was it fifteen?—

councilmen into swearing he'd been at the meeting that night. He could easily do that of course, because they were all undoubtedly dope-takers or undetected murderers. Or maybe they were just a little soft in the head, like a certain private detective seemed to be getting. I scowled into my beer. A vast shape loomed beside me.

'You don't like the drink, there's plenty other places in town.'

I looked up at the uncompromising figure of Gil Randall. Inwardly I groaned. Outwardly I said:

'Hello, Gil. Sit down and have a drink or something.'

'Thanks.'

He lowered his vast frame carefully into the opposite seat. A moment ago I'd been alone in an empty booth. Now I was in a booth full of Randall, and I felt as though I were being squeezed out. It was claustrophobic. He placed two hands like canoe paddles flat on the table between us.

'I'm bushed,' he announced. 'A beer will do fine.'

I didn't say anything. It isn't that I don't like Randall. In fact when you consider that he's a city police officer and I'm just a man with a renewable licence, we get on well enough. What worries me about the guy is his brain. It's like a rapier, flashing here and there, only rapiers destroy things. Randall's brain doesn't do that, it builds things up. Things like facts and opinions, statements, impressions, records and theories. If Randall ever forgot a thing in his whole life, I never heard about it. On top of that I always figure he starts off with an unfair advantage. That sleepy, heavy face belonged on a punch-drunk ex-fighter. His body too, an untidy heap of man that seemed to be dragged around only with a concentrated physical effort. That was a phoney as well. When he chose, Randall could move like a ballet dancer, swift and certain. His rank was only Detective-Sergeant, but that was no knock to his ability. He was a Homicide Detail Officer, Rourke's right hand, and the penny-pinching administration of our fair city couldn't afford to run two lieutenants in the detail. I happened to know he'd been given more than one offer of promotion elsewhere in the department, but he preferred to stay sergeant and stick with Rourke.

I waved a hand to Sam to rustle up some beer and looked across at my sudden guest.

'You just drop in here for a beer?' I queried.

He smiled broadly.

'I like a beer,' he dodged. 'Food is good here too, they tell me.'

'I'm eating,' I advised him. 'The beer is on me. You want food, that's when you start using your own money.'

'You're such a tightwad, Preston,' he grumbled. 'Ah, thanks, Sam.'

Sam set down two beers and pushed a plate in front of me.

'Best in the house, Mr. Preston. Hi, Mr. Randall.'

It smelled wonderful, it looked wonderful. I cut off a piece of the meat and pushed it in my face. It was wonderful.

'Wonderful, Sam,' I acknowledged.

He nodded, pleased, and went away.

'How you coming on the Capone killing?' queried Randall softly.

'That one? Oh, nothing to tell. I'm beginning to doubt she's really the girl I'm looking for,' I told him.

He nodded, removed a few peanuts from the bowl by his hand, slid them into his mouth.

'So you made yourself unpopular for nothing, huh?'

I made a pretence of chewing on the food, delaying a reply until it was swallowed.

'I'm unpopular?'

'Come, come, Preston. A shade too much astonishment there. You're overdoing it. You never saw the day you weren't unpopular with a whole lot of people. Why should today be any different?'

'I thought you meant I was unpopular with some new ones,' I mumbled.

'The guy who runs the Peek-a-Boo, the pig-pen where the girl used to work, he don't like you at all. Name of Vander.'

I shrugged.

'That's tough. I was crazy about him.'

'Really? He's not my type at all. Say, you get out to the ball-park much these days?'

I've had Randall in my hair too long for his abrupt conversation switches to throw me any longer. I talked about the Buffaloes, the boys whose exploits were the source of endless infuriation and embarrassment to the ball fans of Monkton City. Then we talked about Cuba. By the time I was through with the food we'd covered most things from Sam's beer to the next gubernatorial candidates.

'You ready to leave?' asked Randall.

'Yup.'

'I'll walk along with you.'

I paid Sam, winked at the thin nervous-looking man who was arguing quietly with the vast blonde, and accompanied Randall outside.

'Mind if I sit in the car a minute?' he asked.

I minded. Cars can be expensive items and what Randall's bulk would do to the springing didn't bear thought. So naturally I replied:

'Help yourself.'

He climbed in and the Chev rocked as he shifted into position.

'Are we going somewhere?' I queried as I sat beside him.

'No. Just want to talk a minute. Don't like talking in bars. Some day I'll tell you how many guys I put away just because they couldn't keep their mouths shut in bars.'

I stuck an Old Favourite in my face and lit it. The quick flame turned the windshield into a reflector and I looked over the cigarette at the expressionless face of the man next to me. I knew it would be useless to try to hurry him. When he was ready to talk, he'd talk.

'Gonna give you some private information, save you a lotta trouble.'

'And?'

He chuckled richly.

'Does there have to be an "and"?'

'There's always an "and",' I asserted.

The wide shoulders heaved.

'It's a hard world, Preston. O.K., there's an "and".'

I nodded.

'Natch. Let's hear it.'

'Like I said, I'm going to do you this favour. And,' he emphasised the word, 'then you are going to do one for me. Well, not just me. The department, Rourke especially.'

'Do I get a choice?'

'Of course,' he tried to sound aggrieved. 'It's up to you. You can choose whether we do each other a favour or not. Like a trade.'

'Some trade,' I snorted. 'I don't even know what you're holding.'

'So gamble,' he advised. 'You'll never live big if you don't take a little chance now and then.'

I chewed on it. At least I pretended to. I knew very well I was going to do whatever it was Randall wanted.

'All right,' I said wearily. 'Which one is the short straw?'

'Pessimist. Now, this favour I promised. You're wasting your time trying to tie in this Ruby Capone with that bond-skip case of yours. Fact is, we know where those two are, the man and the girl. They're across in Nevada. They haven't been picked up because the police there are waiting to be led to where the dough is. Seems the love birds don't have it with them, and while it will be fine to put the arm on them, it'll feel kind of empty unless the money is recovered too. So you are kind of off-target, hoping Ruby Capone is the girl in the case. Good favour?'

I nodded. From Randall's point of view it was a real favour. He didn't have to tell me the story, and there were plenty of guys who would have thought it a load of laughs to let me go on poking around as long as I liked, knowing all the time I was up a blind alley. It was hardly Randall's fault that I would get no advantage from what he'd told me. If it was anybody's fault it was mine, since it was my own idea to feed the tale to John Rourke in the first place. So I was at a net profit of exactly nothing on the Randall favour. It looked as though I was going to wind up with a large deficit by the time I'd heard what he wanted in return.

'Thanks, Gil. I appreciate it. What do I do for you?'

'Well now, this little thing we want you to do for us, is kind of a bigger favour than the one we did for you. But that is only fair I guess, since the whole trade was our idea?'

'Just how short a straw did I draw?'

'I'll tell you about it. The Vice Squad have been a little bit worried about the increased business the drug-pedlars seem to be doing around the town. Don't tell me this isn't exactly news, because I know it. There was this idea somebody had about trying to plant an undercover operator, try to get at the organisation from inside. A user if necessary. So they did this. This operative came from another town, started work. It was going great too till the other night. Somebody knocked off our agent. It was a woman, by the name of Lola Wade.'

He paused to let me digest it, and I was glad of the rest. To say that Randall had surprised me would have been a mild description of the way my mind was jumping around.

'The broad from the Peek-a-Boo?' I queried.

'The same,' he confirmed. 'Only she was no broad. She was a damned brave woman. On top of that she was police, and somebody killed her. We don't sit by when that happens, Preston.'

He didn't need to tell me that. One thing the police get angry about in a personal way is the killing of a fellow-officer. Add to that the

153

fact that the officer was a woman, and I could guess just how incensed the Monkton P.D. would be.

'This couldn't have been known to many people,' I muttered.

'No,' he agreed. 'Not many. In fact the only ones who knew anything about it till yesterday was the chief himself and the Captain of the Vice Squad. Yesterday, when they killed her, it was different. They sent for Rourke and told him just what kind of homicide he had on his hands, and they O.K.'d for him to tell me. So it still isn't exactly on the front pages.'

'You said, "when they killed her",' I reminded him. 'Does that mean you're certain it was a mob killing?'

'Fairly certain,' he told me. 'Not just a killing. Way we see it, this is a mob execution.'

'I see. You're not telling me all this because you like to gossip. What comes next?'

He rubbed a reflective finger along the windshield.

'Next comes the bit I don't much care about. I got nothing personal against you, Preston, at least no more than against anybody else who interferes in police business and doesn't have a badge. I just don't like the idea of bringing in help from outside.'

Delicately, I said:

'And the help that's to be brought in from outside. That's me?'

He nodded.

'That's the general idea. Before you start getting all excited, let me tell you the way the cards are stacked. Officer Wade was producing results. In a few weeks she's been able to give us a rough picture of the way the narcotics are handled here in Monkton. We know the main agents, the import company if you like, we know a few pushers and where they do the pushing. But we haven't got all we want yet. Somehow the money boys got on to Wade, and they took care of her the only way they knew. With what we have we can put the arm on a few people, get a few convictions. It will annoy the mob, maybe even be a temporary inconvenience, but it won't amount to a hell of a lot in the long run. The whole rotten racket will go on just the same. So we need another Wade. Where do we get one? Anybody new who turns up around any of those guys is going to get rubbed out for sure, just as an insurance policy. We couldn't get a police officer within a mile of the Peek-a-Boo Club, not with his heart still beating.'

He stopped talking for a moment and looked at me sidewise.

'So we have to think of something else,' he continued, after it dawned on him that I wasn't going to make it easier for him.

'What else can we do? Can we approach some of the lesser fry, talk 'em into a stool-job for reward money? Nah. There isn't one of those guys in such a hurry to get dead. You can bet the heat is on inside the organisation. They'll all be watching each other so hard they couldn't put on clean underwear without everybody else knowing. Where would you say that leaves us, Preston?'

Reluctantly, very reluctantly, I said:

'It would seem to me, if I was sitting where you're sitting—and I wish I was—that what you need is somebody to take Lola Wade's place. Somebody who's already known to the operation. Whether they like him or not isn't important. They know him, and whatever else he might be, he's not the law, they know that much. I'd say you needed somebody like that.'

'I'd say that you say right,' he confirmed. 'Let's see if either one of us can think up who might wear that suit.'

'This is kind of a rough ride,' I protested. 'It seems to me you guys take a helluva lot for granted, you and Rourke. I'm trying to dream up one good reason why I should voluntarily walk in on those people and get what Lola Wade got.'

'Come on,' scoffed Randall. 'Nothing terrible is going to happen to you. They've seen you before, you're not police. Maybe they think you're a little bit of a nuisance, maybe even a real pain in the neck. But you don't matter, you're not really important to them. All is gonna happen to you, if you annoy them enough, they'll probably drag you up some alley and give you a little working over. Big strong feller like you, you'll be up and around in a week.'

'If they don't work me over with a hatchet,' I pointed out. 'These guys are in it for real.'

'Sure,' he agreed. 'But this isn't the thirties. You're not messing with a bunch of gun-happy farmhands. Killing these days is a big decision, and there has to be a first-class reason behind it. Believe me, Preston, this is my business. Nobody would get a clearance to have you knocked off, you don't rate that high.'

Although that was intended as a reassurance I found myself oddly affronted. Suddenly it seemed childishly important that I should rate highly enough to be eliminated. How perverse can you get? To Randall, I observed:

'That's as maybe, as things stand at the moment. If they thought I was the new-style Lola Wade, things'd be different quick enough.'

'True, true. But then, we have confidence in you.'

'Confidence?' I was pleased. 'Well, this is a new attitude of mind for you boys.'

'Not really,' he contradicted. 'The confidence lies in the fact we think you're just sneaky enough not to let those guys find out what you're really up to.'

'Thanks for the confidence.'

I sat brooding behind the wheel. Randall's proposition had two sides to it. On the credit side, it was heaven-sent. Here I was digging around on the outside of the Ruby Capone death, very much alone. The man from homicide was offering me a golden opportunity to get closer to the centre of it without exciting police interest in why I should continue my poking around in that direction when I knew from official sources Ruby could not possibly be the girl I had pretended to hope she was. Too, there was the further advantage that if I got myself in a jam there'd be plenty of help coming from the department. That took care of the credit side. On the other hand was the unlovely prospect of trying to buck the dope-traffic from the inside, and this was a most unhealthy way of passing the time. A very high percentage of all the killings in this country arise in some way or other from contact with the merchandise. Narcotics is not just a criminal activity, it's more. It's a multi-million dollar organised enterprise, and nobody and nothing is allowed to place it in jeopardy. If anybody had the slightest reason to suspect what I was up to, I'd be on the next slab to Lola Wade before I could blink. Randall didn't interrupt my thinking. He thought I was weighing up what he'd said, and I was thankful he couldn't read my thoughts at that moment. Finally I sighed,

'What do I have to do?'

'Knew you'd see it our way,' clucked Randall. 'As for what you do, I don't know.

This isn't really our party, the Vice boys are still running it. You be home tonight late, around midnight, they'll be in touch.'

Randall wasn't the man to waste the taxpayers' money. Once he'd sold me the idea he opened the door to get out. As if it suddenly came to mind, he turned back and said:

'You help us nail those people who killed Officer Wade, Preston, and we'll remember it a long time.'

I made no reply, merely nodded. He clambered out and slammed the door. I gave the starter some action and headed for home. It looked as though things might start to get rough.

CHAPTER TEN

I let myself into the apartment at Woodside and closed the door, flicking down the switch at the same time. Immediately I froze where I was. Somebody had been here, could still be here. There was a faint but unmistakeable smell of cigar smoke in the air. I stayed tight, listening, staring rapidly round the place. Then I heard a noise from the bedroom. It was a soft, slithering movement, as if somebody was trying to move very quietly. Gently, scarcely trusting myself to breathe, I eased across the room to the drawer where the .38 lay waiting. When it was safely in my hand I almost whooped with relief. Quietly still, but with a whole lot more confidence, I went over to the door of the bedroom. Then in one movement I flung it inwards and pulled myself wide of the opening. Nothing happened, but the noise was close now. I slid the corner of my face around the jamb, then I put the gun quickly aside.

Rose Schwartz was walking towards the open door. Scarcely walking that is. Dragging one foot painfully after the other, her tall spiked heels making contact with the carpet as she inched along. Her face was a death mask, all make-up standing out in vivid life-imitation on a dying face. Her eyes were glazing fast and a thin trickle of blood ran down from her lower lip where her teeth had bitten into the flesh with the concentrated effort of movement. Rose had to get to that door, get to me. I don't think she was even aware I was standing in front of her, not four feet away. For her, existence was a fundamental question of forcing one of those pathetic high-heeled pumps after the other. Her breathing was a series of racking gasps.

I didn't touch her, didn't go near. Rose was trying to do something, I couldn't tell what. But I knew the whole of her last remaining strength was directed into the effort. If I side-tracked her, claimed her attention at all, the act of turning her mind away from the

160

objective might kill her. Her outstretched arm was close, and I moved away to let her pass. That was when I saw it.

Her back was a bloody ragged mess. Thick dark blood oozed slowly from three blackened holes where large-calibre bullets had ripped their vicious path into her. Somebody had stood very close to her to put that lead in Rose's back, otherwise at least one of the heavy slugs would have gathered impact enough to pass clean through her.

I felt inhuman, standing there watching that ruined and dying body shuffle past. But I told myself that was just sentiment. There was nothing anybody could do for this girl. She was as good as dead already. And dying, there was something she wanted to do, something she had to do. It wasn't for me to stop her last act in this life.

Rose paused and swayed. For a moment I thought she'd go down but after a second one of her feet moved forward again and the pitiful progress recommenced. I knew I ought to be searching the apartment to see whether the killer was still around, but I couldn't take my eyes away from her. Anyway I thought it was unlikely the guy was still around. If he had been he would have put another bullet in her to prevent any last-minute action which could finger him.

At first it seemed she might be heading for the door, then I realised it had to be the telephone. She never made it. Quite suddenly her strength was all gone. Sinking to her knees she gave one low shuddering cry and fell forward. Her outflung arms knocked over the bureau where the telephone stood, and the instrument fell to the floor close to her body. The receiver fell off the cradle, buzzing angrily. I let it lie while I checked quickly through the rest of the apartment but there was no sign of anybody. Whoever had killed Rose Schwartz would be a long way off by this time.

Crossing to the body I picked up the bureau and replaced the telephone. My mind was working like a computer, but all I was producing was blank tape. I looked down at the bundle of sprawling flesh and bones that had been Rose Schwartz. She hadn't done much with her life anybody could be proud of, but she had a right to a better finish than this. Then I noticed something underneath one of her hands. Gently I inserted a finger beneath the palm and pulled a piece of paper free. She must have been carrying it the whole time, and dropped it as her hand relaxed in death.

I smoothed it out and found it was an ordinary scrap of memo paper. On it was pencilled a telephone number. A Vale City number. I stuck the phone against my face and asked for the number. Whoever answered was due for a lot of explaining.

There was an insistent rapping at the door.

'Open it up. Police.'

Damn. Quickly cradling the telephone I crossed to the drawer and put the .38 away. Then I stuffed the piece of paper in my pocket and went to receive my visitors.

They came in fast, guns ready. There were two of them, uniformed men, probably a prowl-team.

'I was just calling you,' I told them.

The fat one sniffed and kept his gun pointing at me. The other took one look at Rose's body, sucked in his breath, and searched quickly through the other rooms. Then he holstered the heavy automatic, knelt beside Rose and touched her.

'Warm,' he announced.

Sniffer nodded, as though that's what he'd expected. His partner lifted the telephone, barked into it quickly, then hung up and turned to me.

'Let's have the story,' he snapped. 'Who are you?'

I told him who I was.

'And her?'

He jerked a thick thumb over his shoulder.

'She goes by the name of Schwartz, Rose Schwartz. You'll find the Vice Squad know something about her.'

Sniffer groaned.

'Oh, no. Another tee-vee student. I'll bet you watch Night Cop all the time.'

The slimmer man ignored this.

'Why'd you kill her?'

'I didn't kill her,' I explained patiently. 'She'd been shot before I got here.'

'This your apartment?'

I confirmed that it was.

'She live here with you?'

'Look, officer,' I said placatingly, 'I know the way this looks, but if you'll just wait till the Homicide boys get here, they'll tell you who I am and that this is nothing to do with me.'

'Will they, now? And just how are they supposed to know that? You mean one of them walked in here with you, found the body, and now he's gone off looking for a policeman? Brother, I don't care if you're the mayor's father. You are in a king-sized jam.'

I shook my head.

'Nuts,' I told them.

Sniffer growled angrily and waved the gun.

'How'd you like to resist a little arrest?' he asked nastily.

Suddenly I didn't like him. It wasn't right that we should be standing there arguing while Rose was lying a few feet away. To Sniffer I said softly,

'Try it, fat boy. Just try any of that jazz on me and I'll wrap that heater round your windpipe.'

His face mottled with rage. I knew I hadn't any business to be needling him the way I was. He was just a man holding down a badge, but I was feeling a sense of mounting frustration

164

and impotent anger because of what had been done to Rose. And right in my own apartment. It had to mean one of two things. She'd either come to me for some reason and they'd caught up with her, or else she'd been brought deliberately so they could kill her where I'd be sure to find her. In other words it could be a lay-off signal. What I ought to be doing was tearing the town apart with my teeth, not standing in useless argument with these well-meaning but unenlightened defenders of the law.

The fat one was about up to boiling point. His partner said:

'Take it easy, Reed. We'll cool this character down a little, later.'

'There isn't going to be any later,' I told him. 'Look, you seem to belong to the same species as me. Mind telling me how you got here so fast? The girl only died a minute before you banged on that door.'

He pondered this, weighing his reply against any possible use I might make of it later. Me, or some smooth-tongued crime lawyer.

'Squeal call,' he finally announced. 'Guy in the next apartment said he thought he'd heard shots in here.'

'Next apartment,' I repeated. 'You got the number?'

'Sure, we got the number,' protested Sniffer. 'Whatsa matter, this is our first pinch or something?'

I ignored that, and continued talking to the slim one.

'You talked with this guy, this neighbour?'

He shook his head.

'What chance did we have. If somebody starts making Wild West we don't have any time to chat with the neighbours.'

'You have time now,' I pointed out. 'Go and fetch this law-abiding citizen.'

'The nerve of this guy,' spluttered Sniffer. 'You think we're—'

The other man cut him short.

'Check it, Reed. I'll watch this man. He isn't going anywhere.'

The fat one wavered. He looked at us in turn, puzzlement wide on his heavy features. Then he put the gun away.

'Ah,' he said disgustedly.

Then he went out.

'O.K. to smoke?' I asked.

The remaining officer eased his own weapon in the shiny black holster.

'What brand?' he surprised me by asking.

'Old Favourites,' I returned.

He nodded with satisfaction.

'Then it's O.K. for us to smoke.'

I grinned, took out the pack and handed him a cigarette. As we puffed the white tubes into life I asked him:

'Why'd you do that?'

'Send Reed out?' he queried. Then, when I nodded to show that's what I'd meant, 'He was getting mad. You shouldn't have riled him up that way. Reed's a good officer, but he'd have whammed into you in another minute.'

I fanned twin plumes of grey smoke from my nostrils.

'Why would that worry you?'

'It wouldn't,' he assured me. 'Just I'm not satisfied with this set-up here. It's screwy. When I went through the joint just now I didn't find any gun. Also the place is so quiet it don't seem natural. These are mighty thick walls you got here. I don't see how this neighbour could hear a gun loud enough to know that's what it was. Through these walls a gunshot would sound like somebody dropped a book in the next room.'

I warmed to this man. A thinker, even if he did smoke my cigarettes.

'There's a gun,' I informed him. 'In that drawer to your left.'

He looked at the drawer casually.

'I've got a buck says it hasn't been fired.'

He slid the drawer open, hefted the .38 and sniffed at it. Then he shrugged, dropped the weapon back in the drawer and pushed it shut. He was one of the coolest policemen I'd run across. Trying not to sound too impressed I said:

'What do you make of it all?'

'I dunno,' he admitted. 'It's screwy. Whether you killed this Miss Schwartz or not is as maybe. One thing is for sure. If we're

167

going to convict you for it, the Homicide Detail is going to have to work extra shifts. I've seen a lot of killers in my time, and a lot of other guys we thought could be killers. Some of them reacted the way you did just now when the badges arrived. With that kind it drops two ways. The guy is either innocent, or else he's guilty, but if guilty, he's smart cunning guilty. Not a type we're going to bluster into making a confession. In fact, this I'll tell you, in my service I've seen two such guys get away with it. And both were as guilty as all hell. So, like I was saying, maybe you did this and maybe you didn't. But which way it goes, we ain't going to make any progress with you using Reed's methods.'

'And of course if I didn't do it, I might put up a squawk that would blip to the moon and back,' I suggested.

He grinned faintly.

'I ought to make sergeant next year. You don't imagine I'm going to take any chances with that bigger pay envelope, do you?'

'You'll make it,' I assured him, and I meant it.

There was no time for more talk because at that moment Reed came back. He wouldn't look at me, but to the other officer he said:

'People this side are away on a vacation. That side, there's a dame lives by herself. I had to drag her out of a bath to come to the door. She didn't phone the department. She doesn't like the department. Especially she don't like me.'

He looked and sounded so crestfallen that I didn't even have the heart to laugh. The slim one crushed his cigarette out and nodded.

'So that's it, uh? No neighbour.'

'And that can only mean one thing,' I pointed out. 'The man who called in was not a neighbour. But he did hear the shooting, because he was the one pulling the trigger. And he just wanted me picked up for nuisance value. If I was unlucky you might have kept me locked up all night.'

The slim one pricked up his ears.

'Why would that have nuisance value? What are you going to be doing tonight that would annoy this guy? That would have to mean you know who he is.'

'No, it wouldn't,' I contradicted. 'Anyway, I'm sorry, but I'll save my talking for the homicide boys when they come.'

Even Reed didn't argue with me this time. His experience with the bathing beauty had knocked all the argument out of him for a while. We all stood around for the next little while waiting for the headquarters men to arrive.

Randall was first. He nodded to the prowl-boys, glared at me, went over and looked at Rose. For a long moment he stood over her, memorising every detail of posture and dress. Then he clicked his fingers at the scientific

169

brigade, and the experts moved in, measuring, testing, checking.

Randall walked over to me.

'You're kind of a busy little feller, ain't you?'

His tone was uncompromising and expression unfriendly. I decided it must be a front for the benefit of the watching patrol officers, and made no reply. The sergeant turned to the two uniformed men who'd been first on the scene.

'You boys could have done a better job than you know,' he told them. 'This character has been walking a high wire for a long time around this town.'

They looked pleased at that. Randall nodded encouragingly.

'What's the story here?'

They told him. Each took it in turn, and so far as I could recall they didn't leave out one thing. Randall stared at the ceiling throughout this performance, never interrupting once.

'What about the murder weapon?' he asked, at the end.

Sniffer shrugged.

'No trace. Unless he threw it out the window.'

'Or flushed it down the john,' added Randall caustically. 'Where's your own gun, Preston? And don't say it's at the cleaners.'

The thinner policeman, the one who was bucking for sergeant, opened the drawer and removed my .38. He handed it over to Randall.

'It hasn't been fired.'

'Hm.'

Randall sniffed at it just the same then slipped it into the side pocket of his jacket.

'Let's go,' he said to me.

'Go where?' I countered.

He sighed with exasperation.

'To headquarters, Preston, headquarters. I'm going to book you for something out of all this.'

I jeered at him.

'You haven't got a prayer and you know it. You've heard what your own boys told you.'

'I heard,' he agreed. 'This is your apartment, you know this girl, you were here when she died. That's a good enough package for me to take you in with.'

It was clear from his tone that this was not the night to argue with Sergeant Randall.

'I won't just sue the department,' I warned. 'I'll sue you personally.'

'Nearly all the people who've been going to sue me personally have wound up inside those high stone walls,' he informed me. 'Let's go.'

I walked with him to the door. The two prowl-boys started to follow, Randall turned round.

'By the way, I brought the photographer in my car. Wonder if you boys would mind giving him a ride over to headquarters when he's through here? I don't want to delay the questioning of this suspect here.'

'Sure.'

'Certainly.'

We left the apartment together. Outside Randall said:

'What's this all about, Preston? Who knocked off that girl, and why pick your place to do it?'

'I don't know.' I still wasn't certain where I stood with Randall at that moment. 'She was one of the people I asked about Ruby Capone's death. In fact she's the one who found Ruby's body.'

'I know that,' he asserted grouchily. 'Questioned her myself. You still haven't answered my questions.'

'Because I don't know the answers,' I assured him. 'All I do know is that I told Rose Schwartz if she ever thought of anything that might help me find out more about Ruby she could come and see me any time. So I'm guessing, and let me repeat that guessing, that Rose remembered something. She came to tell me that something, and whatever it was, was important enough for somebody to kill her before she could pass it on.'

'But you don't know who?'

'I don't know who.'

'H'm.'

We strolled slowly along towards the elevator.

'This could be a break, Preston. I think your friend Ruby was mixed up in this narcotics angle up to her ears. I think you poked your nose in more than you knew when you started asking about her. This Schwartz kill might have been an emergency measure, or it might have been deliberate. What I mean, they might have already decided to knock the girl off and picked your place to do it to kind of warn you to lay off.'

'Be easier just to kill me,' I objected.

'Not necessarily. Not if she had to die, anyway. If she was going to be killed, it had to be because she knew something. These guys are not kill-crazy, they kill for reasons, good ones. There'd be no point to having you eliminated, because at this time you don't know anything. Finding the girl there like that might persuade you you'd be better occupied doing something else.'

'Could be.'

We'd reached the elevator now, but Randall made no attempt to push the button. Instead he pulled out my automatic from his pocket and handed it to me.

'You're going to make a break for it,' he said. 'I'll give you two minutes, then start hollering.'

'What good will it do?' I demanded.

'Who knows? If nothing else, it'll help to convince those guys you haven't any tie-in with the department. Somebody may decide it's O.K. to talk to you if you're on the run. How do I know what good it'll do? We don't have any choice. Only a chump policeman could have failed to take you in after what happened back there. And whatever else people might think about me, I'm not supposed to be that dumb. No, I have to put the arm on you, and you have to make a break.'

'I don't like it,' I protested. 'Every flatfoot in the city will use me for target practice.'

Randall's great head moved decisively from side to side.

'Nope. We will make it a "do not shoot" message. There isn't a cop on the force who would dare disobey that.'

I hoped he was right.

'So what's the move?' I assented wearily.

'That meeting I fixed up for you later tonight, that's out now. You call me at the office around midnight and I'll tell you what the latest position is.'

'All right. Do I make my big bust out now?'

'Go ahead. Remember, two minutes.'

I went down the stairs fast. In all, it took me one minute thirty seconds to reach the Chev and start driving. I headed direct to a car-rental service where they didn't know me, parking my own heap in an all-night park first. Then, with a smooth two-tone convertible under me, I drove back out into the night streets.

They had an air of menace about them now, or so it seemed. By this time, every police officer in Monkton would be on the lookout

174

for me, and I felt those keen eyes straining for me in the darkness. If I was going to do any good before one or other of them found me, I'd better get to work. I headed for Conquest Street.

CHAPTER ELEVEN

I turned into Matt's All-Nite Garage and stopped. A kid with grease on his face hurried to the car.

'Somepin' up, mister?'

'No,' I disappointed him. 'Matt around?'

'In the office, I guess.'

He was eyeing the car with love. He didn't want to talk about Matt. He wanted me to tell him the ignition was shot, or something of the kind. Anything that would give him an excuse to get under that hood and ferret around. An enthusiast.

I climbed out.

'Take her in for me, huh, kid?'

'You're staying?'

'I think so. When I talk to Matt I'll let you know.'

I peered in at the lighted window. A familiar figure was hunched over a bench, concentrating on what looked like racing sheets. Gently I opened the door and stepped inside. Without looking round, Matt grumbled:

175

'What was it, another gas and air big-spender?'

'Didn't spend a nickel,' I replied.

He spun round, his homely face creasing into a giant grin.

'Preston,' he cried. 'Long time no see.'

'How are you, Matt?'

We shook hands and I had a look at him. Ten years back Matt Berens had been number one jockey in the state, and many said in the whole country. He made the mistake of many an honest rider, and tried to race against the big money. The big money around the tracks is bad money, and with those guys you toe the line or else. Matt had been lucky. The horse-van that suddenly reversed, pinning him against the wall of a stable, got a wheel stuck in some mud. Instead of being squashed flat, Matt got off with a split skull and every major bone broken. Every nickel he owned was sucked up in hospital bills, and when he finally came out he was flat busted. A few people gathered round to get him out of hock, and he was able to set up in the garage, an old ambition of his. I was one of the lifeboat crew, and Matt Berens is a guy with a long memory.

'I'm in a little trouble, Matt,' I explained. 'Can I stay here a while?'

'What kinda trouble?' he wanted to know.

'You name it, I'm in it,' I replied. 'Half the town is looking for me. I got a beef with the law for one thing, and the bad men are looking

176

for me too.'

He whistled.

'You know what I think about those guys, Preston. The law now, that's a different tune. I never had no trouble with cops.'

'And you're not going to have any now,' I assured him. 'I only want to be here a couple of hours. You can find something needs doing on the car, can't you, take that long? If a customer chooses to hang around, the air is free, isn't it?'

'O.K.,' he decided. 'I'll have Skip take a look.'

He went out. I picked up the battered telephone and asked for a number. After a while there was the sound of the receiver being lifted off at the other end.

'Hallo?'

It was a man's voice and he sounded puzzled.

'Who is this?' I queried.

'Pattison. Who'm I talking to?'

Pattison. I didn't know anybody by that name.

'Maybe I got the wrong number,' I told him. 'I'm trying to make a connection to Vale City.' I called over the number.

'No, you got the number right, mister. But they ain't nobody here, this time of night. 'Cept me, that is. I'm the night-watchman.'

'Ah,' I said it as much to myself as to Pattison. 'Then that isn't the Two Spades

Club?'

'Nah,' he snorted. 'This here's the Handford Construction Company. Take my tip. Have another drink and go home to bed.'

I broke the connection. The number Rose Schwartz had been clutching so hard in her dying moments had been the office number of Walter F. Handford. And Handford had been practically engaged to Jeannie Benson. And Jeannie Benson had become Ruby Capone, whose dead body was found by none other than Rose Schwartz. Only Handford had never heard of Ruby Capone. He said.

I dialled another number. Now I needed some help.

'*Monkton City Globe,*' announced a squeaky female voice.

'Mr. Steiner,' I said.

'What is your business, please.'

I got impatient.

'I murder telephone girls,' I hissed. 'Four this week already. I want to give myself up to Mr. Steiner and the *Globe.*'

She made a noise like a telephone operator who'd had a narrow escape from butchery, then a familiar tired voice said:

'Is that the killer? This is Shad Steiner. What's the story?'

'Shad, it's me, Preston. I need some information in a hurry.'

'Well, well. For once my staff were right. You really are an escaped killer aren't you?

178

Just had the police call on you.'

'Knock it off, Shad. I'm in a jam.'

'You can whistle that in B flat, friend. How about surrendering to the *Globe*. Make a great story. I pay top prices.'

I could picture him sitting in that worn office, enjoying himself.

'Listen, Shad, how often did I ask you for anything?' I queried.

'Offhand I'd say an average of once a week for more years than I care to think about. All right, all right. So one more will notice? What do you want?'

I told him I wanted anything the Vale City papers had on Walter F. Handford. Any scandals, anything at all. Also, full information on his background. Now that Steiner was through with his little joke, I knew I could rely on him for some action. I gave him Matt's number and he promised to call back. Then I sat down and felt around for a cigarette.

Matt came back in.

'This thing with the cops, is it bad?' he demanded.

Matt's an old friend, and I didn't enjoy lying to him.

'Bad enough,' I nodded. 'They think I killed somebody. A dame.'

He nodded. I'd have appreciated it if he'd looked a little more surprised.

'And did you?'

'Of course not,' I snapped. 'But I have a

better chance to prove it out here than I have in a cell.'

He looked at me, thinking but not saying anything.

'Use some coffee?'

'Always.'

Matt nodded and went out, with that curious rolling gait which had been his legacy from a certain horse-van. The boy poked his head round the door.

'Say, you sure it's the carburettor? I can't find a darned thing wrong with it.'

I spread my hands.

'Don't ask me, kid. I just drive it. If the boss says it's the carb, O.K. it's the carb. The inside of one of those things looks like a Boris Karloff picture to me.'

He grinned quickly, nodded, and withdrew.

Matt came back with a steaming jug of coffee, found some battered cups in a cupboard and poured some of the scalding liquid into them.

'What good's it gonna do you hiding in here?' he demanded. 'Sooner or later you gotta leave, anyway. Don't see you're gaining anything.'

I sipped at the coffee, scalded my tongue and said a word. Then I pointed to the telephone.

'That makes me almost mobile,' I told him. 'Making a few calls. I'll settle with you when I'm through.'

'Nah. Guess I owe you and those other guys anyway. Say, you ever see any of that old crowd these days?'

He fell to reminiscing about his great days on the tracks, and I joined in now and then to show I was still awake. Not that it would have mattered to him if I hadn't. Matt is one of those people, he has a subject. Just turn him on and stand back and he can go on for hours at a stretch. He'd been delivering this monologue for the better part of thirty minutes when the phone jangled sharply. He cursed, broke off what he was saying, and picked it up.

'Matt's Garage. Who? Who do you say? Just a minute.'

He clapped a hand over the mouthpiece and looked at me in puzzlement.

'Some guy asking for you. Says to tell you it's the representative from the fourth estate. What's that mean?'

'It means he's just a nutty friend of mine, Matt.'

I took the phone from him and said:

'Hallo, Preston here.'

Steiner's suspicious voice answered.

'Does your friend know you're a fugitive jailbird, and that I'm the editor of a newspaper that doesn't do business with trash like you?'

'That's two questions,' I replied. 'Answer one is yes, answer two is no.'

'Well, so long as you're sure. I've got the

information you wanted. The man hasn't put a foot wrong since he first came to Vale City some years ago. He's in good standing every way, social, political, financial. Unlucky, too. He has this sick wife in a sanatorium.'

'I know about her,' I told him glumly. 'So he doesn't have any vices, eh?'

'Not that we can trace,' he confirmed.

Trying not to sound too disappointed, I said:

'Well, I appreciate the trouble you've taken, Shad. One thing, where did he come from?'

'Wait a minute, I have that down here someplace. Yes, here it is. Place called Larchville, Nebraska.'

'O.K. and thanks again.'

I promised to let him know how things were progressing, then cut the connection. Matt sat in absorbed silence while I got through to Florence Digby at her home. She wasn't amused at being dragged away from her favourite television programme, but quickly cooled down when I told her I was in trouble. I wanted the name of anybody in my own line of business in Larchville, Nebraska. Florence kept me hanging on while she hunted through the reference books. I learned a long time ago that it's a mistake to have all the information locked away in the office. Miss Digby keeps duplicate works of reference at home, and I have some at my own place too. The emergencies when these things are needed

182

don't come very often, but when they come the prudence pays off. Like now.

Within a few minutes she came up with just one name. Larchville had a population small enough for me to feel lucky to find even one guy who could scrape a living out of our uncertain profession. His name was Lasky, Cyrus Lasky, and I wrote down the number. Then I thanked Florence, told her not to worry and asked for long distance. Matt paled at the thought of what all this telephone work was going to cost, and I grinned at him cheerfully while I was being put through. That time of night the lines weren't so busy and it wasn't long before Lasky was breathing down the other end.

I told him who I was and he said how was I and I said fine and he said what could he do for me.

'There's a man here runs a construction company,' I told him. 'Originally he was a Larchville man and I want to know anything you can tell me about him.'

'Name?'

'Walter F. Handford,' I said, speaking slowly and clearly.

There was a pause. I imagined it was while Lasky wrote down the name. I was wrong.

'Handford?' he finally said. 'Tell me, what is it with this Handford? He seems to make quite a stir in your little pool.'

'How do you mean? Do you know him?'

'Nope. Never heard of him till a few months ago. Then I got this enquiry from some dame over there. She was on the same pitch. I'd never heard of him till she asked about him, but now I even have a note of how often he used to shave.'

'Who was the woman who wanted to know?' I asked.

Lasky tutted.

'You should be ashamed, asking me a question like that. I may be just a small town operator, but my ethics come a little bigger than that, Preston.'

Softly, I cursed ethics, and in particular the brand used by Cyrus Lasky of Larchville, Nebraska.

'All right, never mind the dame. What did you get on this Handford. Anything in our line, with meat on it?'

'Nossir, not a thing. Course, I'm not pretending to you I remember all the details, it was several months back. But I do recall it was a very clean, neat record. No blank spaces, if you know what I mean.'

A sense of bitter disappointment came over me. A lot of the thoughts I'd been having needed guilt on Handford's part as a starting point. And it was getting late in the day for new thinking.

'You must have made a file on the man,' I said. 'Do you have your office at home?'

'Nope,' he said flatly. 'And I'm not going

184

down there this time of night, either. I tell you the guy is clean. Tomorrow I'll put it all in the mail, and you can see for yourself. Along with a bill for my services.'

'Don't worry about your money, you'll get it. I don't want to wait for the mail, though. Will you telephone my office and read it out to my secretary?'

'And charge extra?'

'And charge extra,' I confirmed.

'Will do. What's the number?'

I told him the number and gave him Florence's name. He promised to call at nine-thirty a.m., and that was the end of my talk with Mr. Lasky.

Matt had been drinking in the conversation.

'This Handford,' he observed. 'You figure he's the guy really bumped off the dame the cops are trying to nail you for? By the way, Skip has a radio out there. They put on a flash while I was talking to him.'

'Does he know it's me they're looking for?'

He looked pained.

'Be your age, Preston. You think I've gone soft in the head? Anyway you didn't answer me. You figure this Handford did it?'

I shook my head.

'I don't know, Matt. It's a mess, a real mess. An hour ago I thought I had some ideas about it. Now I'm not so sure.'

A quick check told me it was eleven-thirty. I wasn't due to call Randall until midnight. That

185

gave me thirty minutes in which to devote my rapier brain to the unravelling of this simple puzzle which had so far killed three people. After five minutes I knew I wasn't going to get anywhere by just thinking about it. My rapier brain seemed to have become submerged in some sticky substance which was not sympathetic to brilliant thinking.

There was a sound of voices outside. Matt looked through the grimy glass and swung round.

'Cops,' he hissed. 'They usually call round if somebody goes missing, to see whether I've rented out a car. If Skip tells 'em we have a visitor, they're bound to come check.'

'I'll have to blow. Can't get you in trouble, Matt. How do I get out?'

'Through here.'

He heaved at wooden shelving. Behind it was a door.

'Never use it,' he explained. 'Just leads into an alley.'

'Right. Look Matt, at midnight, phone police headquarters. Tell Sergeant Randall I'm at the Peek-a-Boo Club. Got it?'

'Midnight. Randall. Peek-a-Boo. You better git.'

I opened the door and stepped out. Immediately, it closed and I heard the shelves scraping back into place.

Behind me and all over town were the police. Ahead was Vander and the Peek-a-Boo

186

Club. The night air was chilly and I shivered slightly.

Or maybe it wasn't the air.

CHAPTER TWELVE

A narrow opening to the left of the Peek-a-Boo Club led to what was supposed to be a service entrance. As an entrance it no doubt did its share of duty by way of booze deliveries and so forth, but its main purpose in life was to provide a rear exit. When you run a joint like the Peek-a-Boo, you have to take account of the bizarre pastimes of some of the clientele. A method of exit other than through the front door is a desirable extra attraction to be able to offer customers who may wish to split the scene without having to push their way past anybody coming in. Such as an inquisitive police officer. I knew the door would not be locked and I also knew there was no risk of making a squeaky entry. Silence is an essential for a rear door, and the heavy specimen at the Peek-a-Boo proved no exception.

I was inside a narrow, ill-lit passage, the same one as I'd entered on an earlier visit from the further end. There was nobody around as I walked quietly along to Vander's office. Pausing, I listened at the door, but could hear no sound. Then I opened it and stepped quickly inside. Vander was sitting behind his desk reading a newspaper. He looked up irritably, gasped and grabbed for a drawer. I laughed and showed him my police special. He stopped in mid-action, hand seemingly frozen in space a couple of inches from the drawer handle.

'Lay it on the table,' I suggested.

When he saw that I had no immediate intention of firing, he recovered some of his confidence.

'Well, well,' he muttered softly. 'Preston, isn't it? Half the coppers in town are tearing it apart looking for you.'

'That so? Any idea what for?'

I moved to one side of the door as I spoke in case anyone should come in.

'For murder, Preston, that's what for,' he informed me. 'What'd Rose ever do to you?'

'Nothing,' I replied. 'And in return, I did nothing to Rose. I didn't kill that girl and you know it.'

'I only know what the police say, and according to them it's your kill.'

He was watchful, tensed as though expecting something. That could be either a bullet from me, or somebody else joining the party.

'I didn't come here to talk to you about what they think,' I said nastily. 'Came to get a little information.'

'What about?'

'About the queer coincidence that puts three of your girls in the morgue within the space of a few days. Why do you suppose that should be?'

'How should I know,' he shrugged. 'You tell me.'

'All right. The big men in narcotics are using this place as a kind of distribution centre. Have been for months. You don't like it, but you just do as you're told. It isn't your play, because you don't have the guts for that particular trade. To keep trade healthy somebody has to die every now and then, a user, a cop, somebody. And you don't go in for the heavy stuff, so that means you're practically a bystander. But when the big men say they intend to use your place you also don't have the guts to say no, because that could get you dead, too. And you'd be afraid to risk that. So they move in, do what they want to do, slip you a couple of hundred a week for the hire of the hall. How does it sound?'

'It sounds like a bad movie,' he sneered, but there was a whiteness around the eyes which robbed the words of any conviction.

'Keep listening,' I advised. 'To anybody outside you still look like the head man, and as far as running the booze and the girls are concerned, you are. But for the real business, you're just the office boy. Then suddenly, there's trouble, real trouble. One of the girls

189

turns out to be a police officer. That didn't look too good for you with the top men, I imagine, Vander. You hired her, put her where she could get a good view of the operation. They probably didn't think too highly of you, I guess.'

Doggedly, he replied:

'Lola came to me with good reports from the boys up in Fresno. If she was the law, this is the first I've heard of it.'

I grinned.

'But Vander, old friend, nobody mentioned Lola. You've had three girls killed, what makes you mention Lola?'

He bit his lip but didn't answer.

'So, as I was saying, there was this problem about this woman policeman, Lola Wade, as you tell me. Naturally, she has to be eliminated, but these things have to be properly cleared. No rushing around waving a gun, like in the old days. A killing has to be O.K.'d from the top echelon. Then an extraordinary thing happened. One of your other girls died. And not just anyone of them, but your own particular choice. She died from an overdose of H, and again you don't look too good with the big fellows. One thing they can do without is a direct narcotics link with the Peek-a-Boo, and here's your own girlfriend dumps one right in the law's lap. Headquarters in San Francisco must have loved you.'

His fingers had begun a nervous twitching

190

as they lay before him on the surface of the desk.

'I don't know what any of this leads up to,' he jerked out, 'but if you think I did anything to hurt Ruby—'

'No,' I cut in, 'I don't think that. But Ruby died just the same, and that meant no more peddling from here for a while. Police in this town have two major vices from the point of view of people like you. They're smart and they're honest, and if there was even a grain of white powder in this place they'd find it, and you would draw a nice long sentence. Also it would be bad for the trade, a lot of publicity like that. So the big men moved their operation out overnight. They also probably gave you some kind of ultimatum. Clean it up, or they might have to do something about you. You had made two important mistakes and it could cost them a lot of money, and money is the one place those guys are very sensitive.'

There was a knock at the door. Vander's head jerked hopefully towards it. I pointed the .38 towards the door.

'Let 'em in,' I ordered.

'Who is it?' called the man at the desk.

The door opened a foot and what happened then was too fast for me. A hand appeared holding an enormous .45 revolver. The big weapon kicked twice, and Vander half-rising from the table fell forward across it. The door was closing again almost at once. Pulling myself together, I turned and fired. The slug tore its way through the flimsy panelling and there was a hoarse shout of rage and pain from the other side. Standing back I ripped off two more shots, but there was no more sound from beyond the door. Glancing quickly over my shoulder I decided Vander was either dead or very close to it. There was nothing to be done where I was. I had to go through that door.

A bead of cold perspiration ran down my cheek and I suddenly found I was breathing heavily. I moved across until I could see through the partly-open door. Nothing. Then there was a crash as another door was flung open. Quickly now, I peered out into the passage. Ben, the man I'd seen on my last visit, was coming through from the club at the run. He saw me, stopped and dived inside his coat. I shook my head impatiently and pointed the .38 at him.

'Not me,' I snapped. 'Somebody just gunned Vander. I hit whoever it was. Anybody come through the club?'

He wagged his head, uncertain whether to believe me.

'No.'

'Then he must have left by the other door. Come on.'

Together we ran down to the service entrance. We were still a few feet short when it swung suddenly open. A man stood facing us, and we stopped running when we saw the heavy calibre gun in his hand. He was Jammy, the little man in the rainbow-hued clothes who'd beaten up Rose Schwartz so badly. The gun was the one I'd seen shoot Vander, and blood was oozing thickly from his shoulder, which had to be where I'd hit him.

Beside me Ben gasped with sudden fear. Sounding braver than I felt I snapped:

'Drop it, Jammy.'

He looked at me, shook his head in wonderment, then buckled at the knees. Only the frame of the door was holding him up. He coughed then, and a thin rivulet of blood welled from the side of his mouth. With a shuddering sigh he pitched forward on his face. We stood looking down at the red slits in his back where a knife had been rammed cruelly home.

'Insurance,' I muttered.

Ben nodded.

'Looks that way. Let's go check the boss.'

I went back with him to Vander's office. Not because I thought any check was necessary, but because that was where I'd find a telephone.

Ben went to the sprawled figure on the desk.

'Dead,' he announced.

I took out an Old Favourite, and was annoyed to see how my hand shook as I lit it.

'It has to be cops, Ben. You know that.'

He looked at me curiously.

193

'What's it all about? You said something about insurance, and it looked like it to me. But why any of it?'

'Let's call the law,' I evaded. 'We can talk later.'

I picked up the phone from its cradle beside Vander's body.

'Get me the police. Emergency,' I told the operator.

'Somebody mention police?' queried a well-known voice. I put the receiver down as Gil Randall and another man walked in.

CHAPTER THIRTEEN

It was two o'clock in the morning and I was nursing a steaming cup of coffee in the office of the Captain of Detectives, Homicide Detail, Monkton City Police Department. I'd been in the office many times before, but never in such an honoured capacity as to be trusted with one of the city's cups. Rourke himself wasn't around, and I was waiting for Gil Randall who was downstairs making a preliminary report to the ranking duty officer. I was glad of the break. It gave me my first opportunity for a quiet think since the shambles at the Peek-a-Boo Club. It also gave me breathing space in which to try remembering which parts of the mess were already known to the law, which

194

parts I could now safely release, and most important of all, which parts I had to keep locked up in my mind. The last part was also the hardest, because it's one thing to have the intention of withholding information from an experienced interrogator, and quite another to get away with it once the chips are down.

The coffee was good, or maybe I was so tired anything hot would have seemed like nectar. I let my thoughts wander around the events of the past couple of days, looking for something that would give me a lead to the truth about Ruby Capone's death. I'd made a mental note earlier to stop thinking about those other names of hers. They were known only to her father and me, whereas Ruby was a five-minute celebrity around the city. I hadn't made a lot of progress when Randall came in.

'They gave you java?'

He sounded impressed.

'Why not? I'm some kind of honorary policeman tonight, aren't I?'

'Some kind,' he assented grudgingly. 'We wouldn't care to have too many in the department who let a murder happen right under their noses. And then let the killer get away. And then let somebody else nail the killer, and then let *them* get away too.'

I looked up to complain about the testimonial, stopped when I saw the grin on his face.

'Just kidding, Preston. Wasn't much else you

195

coulda done.'

He laid a brown folder on Rourke's desk.

'Well thanks,' I replied. 'Maybe I didn't look too hot, but I told you exactly what happened back there.'

'You told me? Oh, yeah, you did, didn't you? I was hardly listening. This,' he tapped at the folder, 'this is what tells me things. Room measurements, ballistics reports, examining medic's report. This is the stuff. This tells me facts.'

'And what do the facts say?' I tried not to sound sarcastic.

'O.K.,' nodded Randall. 'They say it happened the way you told it.'

Walking to the door he stuck his head out and bellowed.

'How about some coffee in here?'

Then he came back and sat down behind his own desk. The accommodation is not exactly ritzy at the Monkton City P.D. The two top men of Homicide, Rourke and Randall, have to share one ill-lit office which is in bad need of a paint job. Their desks are placed facing each other and the visitor sits in the middle. This gives the visitor a choice. He can either sit facing one of them and feel the other's cold eyes boring into his back, or he can sit half-faced to both, and enjoy the experience of having a crossfire of questions. Tonight I was lucky. Rourke was home in bed, so I sat facing Randall, leaning one arm on the desk.

'What do you think it's all about, Preston?'

'You're the second person to ask me that tonight,' I told him.

'Yeah. Who was the other one and what'd you tell him?'

'It was Ben, Vander's man. I didn't tell him a thing.'

'Good, good,' he clucked. 'Then you won't feel as though you're just repeating yourself. Tell it to me.'

This was the time to be economical with words, I recalled.

'You'll have to remember I only came in halfway through the programme,' I reminded him. 'A lot of this will be just guessing.'

Randall nodded as though half-asleep. I wished he was.

'I'll remember. Guess some.'

'Vander ran the club, a few drinks, a few girls. He's been doing it a long time and you never figured him worth closing up so my guess is it was just what it seemed. A penny-ante girlie-drop.'

'Keep guessing.'

'Somebody got to Vander, told him the quick way to the big money was to push horse—'

'Horse? Please don't use these bar-room expressions in this office. What's horse?'

'Horse, sergeant, is a term used by people in the illicit drug traffic. It means heroin.'

'Every day something new,' he marvelled.

197

'So Vander is sold on the idea. He starts to peddle the powder. In no time our respected Police Department gets wind of it, and an undercover officer is brought in from outside. Unfortunately Vander, or somebody working for him, spots the officer and so there has to be a killing.'

Randall's face hardened as I came to this part, and I hoped my guessing would be good.

'Vander knows Lola Wade is the only real on-the-spot witness the police have. Without her it's unlikely they can make out much of a case against him. On the other hand, if she's murdered, and the police can bring narcotics charges which will be publicised in connection with her death, there's a risk of a homicide charge sticking too. So Vander has a brilliant idea. Let Miss Wade be murdered, certainly, but not apparently because she's a police officer. Have her killed in a way that makes it look as though she was killed, as a result of being what she was supposed to be. A booze-joint clippie with a habit. The idea was all right, but he had to convince the law as well as the public. So he had to think up something extra to sell the idea.'

Randall was stroking a huge palm down the side of his cheek. Suddenly he stopped and said:

'I like this. None of us here were able to agree about why Officer Wade was bumped off in that particular way. A gun or a knife, O.K.

198

But we couldn't agree about the needle routine.'

'If you couldn't agree, I doubt you'll have much respect for my opinion,' I shrugged. 'Still, here's some more guessing. Vander decided to have another killing first. Sort of set the pattern. He picked on one of the girls from the club, Ruby Capone. Ruby was especially suitable. She hadn't any friends in town, no tie-in with any hard guys who might want to make things rough for the killer. She had also the particular qualification that no one would dream Vander was implicated. Because she was Vander's own girl. There were no fights going on, they were like cooing doves, and Vander could produce fifty witnesses to say so if he had to. So he chose Ruby.'

'Tell you something about that Capone dame later,' interrupted Randall. 'Finish your guesswork first.'

I'd have very much preferred to have him tell me whatever it was about Ruby first, but it was his office.

'That was the scheme. Bump off Ruby Capone in this weird fashion with the overloaded needle. Then, next day, give the same treatment to Lola Wade. Same club, same kind of girl, same kind of killing. And not a pro. job either, not the kind of thing a professional would rely on.'

'I'm with you so far. Then what?'

'Then,' I grinned apologetically, 'an

199

interfering guy with a private licence started asking questions about Ruby Capone. I didn't find out a thing worth mentioning, but I was asking questions. There was a man who found Ruby's body, a man named Took. He had to be mixed up in this somewhere, although naturally I didn't know where. Vander thought Took was the kind who might break down under the kind of questions I'd ask him in a sound-proof cellar somewhere. So he decided to get his boy out of town.

'Staged a little fight in his office. It could have worked out either way. Took could have stuck a convenient hole in me somewhere so I'd need to spend a while in hospital. That would have suited Vander very well. As it happened, I got lucky. I broke Took's arm for him. When I did that Vander got all worked up, told Took he was through and to get out of town. It was very impressive.'

'Anybody else see this?' queried Randall gently.

'Oh sure, Ben was there. You can ask Ben.'

'Don't think I won't,' he assured me. 'Breaking arms yet. Go on.'

'Well that got Took out of my reach. But he had a girl, Rose Schwartz. Vander sent this little lover boy Jammy to have a talk with Rose. Jammy talked to her a while, mostly with his feet. He was a real sweet guy and I'm real sorry about what happened to him. Anyway I started to pressure Rose, but she couldn't tell me anything. I was sorry for her, so I gave her a few dollars and put her on a train out of town. That was just before I met you last night.'

'Train? She didn't care for long journeys evidently.'

'I think she either decided there was something she could tell me about Ruby after all, or else somebody saw me take her to the station. It was a local train, she could have been taken off at any whistle stop between here and L.A. Then she came to my apartment either alone, if it was her own idea, or with Vander's killer if it was his. She was killed there to warn me to lay off.'

'Why with a gun?' objected Randall. 'Why not do the needle bit again, leave all the stuff in your apartment and make you the prize suspect for all the killings?'

'That would have been a much smarter move,' I agreed. 'But you have to remember this was an emergency kill. There was no time for fancy arrangements. Rose had to be killed and in a hurry.'

'Suppose she hadn't been on her way back to you? Suppose they did take her off that train? Why would they have to do it and why kill her?'

'I don't know. But it's my guess Rose did know something about Ruby's death, maybe even about Lola Wade's too. They knew she'd been with me a long time. They wouldn't have any way of knowing how much she'd told me already.'

'H'm.' Randall didn't sound convinced. 'Well, since we're only guessing, I suppose it could be. Try the rest of it.'

'Not much more to guess. But it is the big guess this time. I think the big men in the narcotics business were finding Vander a nuisance. When the news broke tonight—last night—about the Rose Schwartz shooting, they finally decided Vander was drawing too much publicity. On top of that, I doubt whether he'd cleared the Schwartz thing with the boys higher up, and you know better than I do they won't tolerate that kind of action until they've given the O.K. I think they decided to get rid of Vander. They told Jammy to do it.'

Randall nodded this time, as if in complete agreement.

'I'm with you on this part of the story. Jammy was sent to knock off Vander, and then some total stranger was brought in to take care of Jammy. Insurance. That is syndicate procedure right down the line. Oh yes, I agree with you. That Jammy kill was a typical mob operation. Funny thing is, they needn't have bothered. Jammy was a mess physically. That slug you put in him would have killed him anyway in another few hours.'

'Good.'

I felt no remorse at all, just a satisfaction that I'd managed to get one back for Rose

Schwartz.

'Don't cry all over the furniture,' implored Randall.

'You were going to tell me something about Ruby Capone,' I reminded him.

'Oh yeah.'

He stopped talking as the door opened and a uniformed policeman came in with a tin tray.

'Ah, thanks. This'll hit the spot.'

I had to wait for the information about Ruby, while the fragrant coffee hit Randall's spot, wherever that was.

'Man, that is better. That is very much better.'

He smacked his lips with satisfaction. I've never heard him make such a near-human sound before.

'Capone,' I prodded.

'Sure, yes, Capone. She was an odd one, no?'

'Odd enough to get herself bumped off. Otherwise she didn't seem anything special to me,' I replied carefully.

'That's what I mean. She didn't seem special to anybody. But she was a little bit special just the same. Just a two-dollar hooker wouldn't you have said?'

'I don't get all the mystery,' I said peevishly. 'But if you want to play games, O.K., she seemed like a floozie to me.'

'Exactly, to you and practically everybody else. Everybody but Lola Wade. That was a first-class police brain we lost there. She felt from the start there was something unusual about Capone. Even asked the department to try digging something up about her. It was a waste of time, there wasn't any record or like that. Not that it was very surprising. They come in out of the night, these dames. Every town a new name, a new story. We can never check one third of them out. Course, you have to remember the Vice boys were the ones in contact with Wade, not this outfit.'

'You told me before,' I reminded him. 'So there was nothing on Capone?'

'Uh uh. But Wade still had this stray feeling about her. She broke into Capone's apartment, if you can call it that. That made her even more suspicious. Ruby Capone looked like the other dames, talked like them, dressed like them. But her personal stuff was all out of character. Women have a strong nose for things like that, and with a police woman it's a highly trained instinct.'

'She seems to have gone to a lot of trouble over just an idea,' I suggested.

Randall looked at me witheringly.

'What do you keep in that head? I'm not talking about some nosy dame. I'm talking about a police officer who was doing a highly dangerous undercover job. Officer Wade was gambling with her life, and she couldn't take chances with anything that looked the slightest bit unusual. Do you want to hear the rest?'

'I'm sorry,' I apologised. 'Yes, I want to hear the rest.'

'Then shut up, and listen. Wade was getting all worked up by this time. Capone was Vander's girl, everybody knew. She didn't play games with any of the customers. Just coaxed 'em into spending their money, but anything else was out. And yet everything in her apartment indicated a different kind of girl. A decent girl, if the expression is familiar.'

He cocked an inquiring eyebrow in my direction.

'I've heard it before,' I admitted.

'So she thought she'd nail this Capone, have it out with her. One night she waited outside till she came home. Vander wasn't with her. Wade pushed her way in and acted very excitable with Capone. Oh, one thing I forgot to mention. In the apartment Wade had found almost two ounces of horse—'

'—heroin?' I queried gently.

Randall sniffed.

'I don't know whether you have any idea of the market value of that stuff, but two ounces is a hell of a lot of happy dust for anybody to have at one hit. Wade's theory was, and it proved to be right, that this Capone wasn't on the stuff at all. She was buying it like everybody else, then taking it home and just storing it. So this night, as I was saying, Lola Wade shoved her way into Capone's place and started cutting up. She told Capone she knew she wasn't a junkie and that she was a phoney all round. Accused her of being a police spy, which was kind of a cool idea, and said she was going to expose her to Vander. Capone begged her to keep to herself what she'd found out. She wasn't working for the police she said, it was a private matter. Wade wasn't going to be convinced, then Capone offered her a thousand dollars to keep her mouth shut. Wade said it was no deal, and what good was the grand if she was in jail? Capone was pretty desperate by that time, and she said O.K., she'd tell Wade the score, but she'd kill her if she spread the story round. She wasn't just using words either. Wade said the girl sounded as if she meant it. So she pretended to get scared and said she'd swear never to repeat it. Then she got Capone's story. The girl had a brother once, she said. The kid was no wilder than most boys of his age, but he got a habit and he went from bad to worse. Turned into a regular little gangster. She tried everything, even begging the big shots to let him alone. One of the head men said he'd see what he could do about it, for a price. The price was Capone. She was a girl from a very strict home, she told Wade. It wasn't an easy bargain for her. But she paid, she moved in with the guy, and he promised to do what he could about the brother. Well, you can guess the rest. The big shot had his fun with the girl, didn't lift a finger to help the brother. Finally the kid was killed in a hold-up. Capone nearly went out of her head, but Mr. Big just told her to pack up and get out.'

'Sounds like a real wise feller,' I said softly.

Randall shrugged.

'You know what chance you got of doing business with lice like that. This Ruby Capone just hadn't seen enough of the world to know what to expect. Only she didn't do a dive off a bridge, like plenty have done. She moved out one night from San Francisco and came here to Monkton. With a scheme. The scheme was to move in at one of the branches of the business. She already knew a great deal about the set-up in San Francisco. She knew names and places. A girl with less sense in her head would have marched into police headquarters and started talking her head off. The police would have had a good solid case and they'd have won a few convictions. But Capone's life wouldn't have been worth a plugged nickel. She'd get police protection of course, but that wouldn't go on for ever. After a few months, even a year, the syndicate would get to her. Even supposing she went to another town, she'd never feel safe. She knew too much about the size of the organisation to think she could hide anywhere. So she came here about six months back, took up a new name— Capone wasn't her real name, maybe we'll never know that now—and got herself in with Vander. She was going to play along for a few months, give the boys in San Francisco a chance to forget about her. And she wouldn't be wasting her time here, either. She intended to follow through the delivery system from 'Frisco. That way she ought to be able to turn over to the law a complete story on the stuff from the moment it came off the docks up in the Bay until the needle went in somebody's arm down here. Not a big operation at this end, but it would all go to making a more watertight case against the top operators when the time came.'

'She was a smart girl,' I observed. 'But I don't see why she should tell all this to Officer Wade. That doesn't sound too bright to me.'

'No, I'm telling it badly. All this stuff about getting evidence and so on, that came out after Wade decided to tell her who she was. She thought she could use the girl, and the Vice Squad gave her the green light. So, I'm sorry Sherlock, but your little theory about Vander knocking off Ruby Capone to cover up the important murder of Lola Wade, just won't hold water. Here in the department we think he was wise to Capone as well as Wade, and that was the reason she had to go.'

I nodded as if in agreement. Ruby Capone had certainly thought up a beautiful story for Lola's benefit. Even after her death it was still a beauty. Of itself it served to explain to the police why she had died, and relieved me of any guilty feeling about concealing from them what I knew.

'Poor kid,' I muttered. 'I mean Capone. All that trouble to make sure the top men couldn't catch up with her, then she gets bumped off by a nothing like Vander. There doesn't seem to be a lot of justice in the world, eh, Gil?'

'Oh, I don't know,' he said ponderously. 'There's irony there, too. Don't forget that by killing her Vander thought he was protecting the important people in San Francisco as well as himself. Their way of expressing gratitude was to send Jammy to see him with a .45. And there's more. Ruby Capone had already given Officer Wade a whole lot of invaluable material, probably enough for a major prosecution up in 'Frisco. So the girl's efforts weren't all wasted.'

'Well, that's good news at least,' I agreed. 'One thing puzzles me still. If Vander was going to kill Capone, or have her killed, whichever it was, what was all the business about taking her up to her apartment after she was dead? Seems to me that's taking a terrible extra chance on being seen. Unnecessary.'

Randall wagged his head up and down.

'Been wondering about that myself. We'll probably never know the real story now, but I figure it this way. Vander for some reason wasn't able to pick the time and place she died. Maybe he suddenly found out she was going to the police, or maybe they had a fight and she came out with it all. Who knows, exactly? But

I'm assuming Vander found out quite suddenly that she had to die, and that it had to be done quickly. You give me a better explanation, I'm listening. But that's how it sets up with me. Once it was done he had to get rid of her, and not to some alleyway either. That would have been the end of his dream that we would swallow it as the work of a deviate. The place for a corpse like that to turn up is indoors. And the only indoors that fitted the appearance he wanted to present was the girl's own apartment.'

It was thin. Randall knew it was thin, and he knew I'd think so too. What he didn't know was how glad I was he was prepared to accept the weak spots having regard to the way the rest of it dovetailed in. It meant he was satisfied with the general pattern, and in turn that meant he wasn't going to spend a great deal more time prying into Ruby Capone's history.

'Could be,' I said slowly. I didn't want to seem too anxious about it, and my comment seemed to suit Randall.

'I know it isn't according to the book,' he observed. 'But what do you want? We know the most of it, and a few little pieces are always left sticking out of the drawer. You know that, Preston.'

'I know it. Say, how about breaking official silence on a confidential matter?'

'For you, nothing. You know that, too.'

'C'mon, Gil. Satisfy my curiosity. After all I could have got killed a few hours back, doing all this special undercover man bit for you guys.'

'Heart-breaking,' he told me laconically. 'What's the question?'

'It's this big shot Ruby told Lola Wade about. The guy with the lovely disposition, the one she was out to get. Who was it?'

He inspected me carefully, as if he'd never seen me before.

'Well, I guess it'll do no real harm to tell you. The man was Rudy Benito.'

And of course, I'd known that it had to be. I didn't understand it, couldn't fathom why Jeannie Benson, after years away from Benito, should suddenly do what she'd done. Become Ruby Capone, live like a cheap hustler and try to work up a case against her own father. Randall was satisfied, naturally. He knew the whole thing, the wild brother, the big shot who betrayed the trusting sister, and all that East Lynne. It was a good story, and it had the additional conviction that the girl called Ruby Capone had been murdered, there was no gainsaying that. The only thing wrong with it was, it just wasn't true. But this was no time for me to be enlightening the department on that point.

'He's big enough,' I conceded. 'And thanks for telling me.'

'Not at all,' waved Randall magnanimously.

'We gave it to the press boys over an hour ago.'

I grimaced to show he'd made his point. Then he said:

'Well, looks as though there's nothing in this for you, huh? You better start looking around for some work that'll bring in the gravy.'

'Guess so,' I admitted. 'Since you've been so open-handed with the inside stuff about Benito, does that mean you have a warrant out for him?'

'Not us, no. The San Francisco P.D. issued a warrant yesterday morning.'

So that was what Benito had been doing when I saw him the previous day in Monkton. The man was holed up. Again I was thankful Randall couldn't see inside my head.

'They pick him up yet?' I queried.

The huge head jerked quickly sideways.

'Not yet. But a guy that big, we'll get him pretty quick if he doesn't skip the country. Too well known, got too much money, made too many enemies. It shouldn't be hard.'

'Good.'

I got up and buttoned my coat.

'Special Officer Preston signing off, if that's O.K. with you, sergeant.'

'Yeah, it is getting late, isn't it? Almost three a.m. There'll be an inquest naturally on Vander and Jammy. I'll let you know when it is.'

'Thanks.'

I went slowly down the stairs. I was thinking

about the big excitement the papers would make next morning. With the build-up I knew I'd get from the department I would look pretty good in the rags. To everybody except me. And perhaps Benito. And perhaps also, a third party. Somebody who knew something nobody else did. The death of Ruby Capone could be explained in the way Randall had spelled it out, otherwise Randall wouldn't have tolerated the theory. But I didn't think it was the right explanation. I thought there had to be something else, somebody else. Somebody who would probably read the story with his breakfast coffee, smile a wide smile, and sit around waiting to die of old age. The hell of it was, I couldn't think of a single thing I could do to prevent it.

CHAPTER FOURTEEN

The telephone shrilled and I cursed. What did I have to do to get service in this town. It had been after four in the morning when I finally took my troubles to bed with me. I'd had the good sense to take off the receiver, warn the operator what I was doing, and leave it lying on the table. That guaranteed me uninterrupted sleep. I planned on sleeping till about eleven and here it was only—pulling a hand free of the sheets I squinted at my

213

watch—only nine-forty. And how in hell did the telephone get back on the hook?

My mind a turmoil of evil thoughts I stumbled across to the table.

'Well?' I grunted.

The crisply-laundered voice at the other end belonged to Florence Digby.

'Are we grumpy this morning?' she asked. 'According to the newspapers you ought to be feeling quite pleased with yourself.'

It was evident from la Digby's inflections that her opinion of me, built up over the years, was not to be swayed by some yarn in a tabloid.

'Late night,' I replied, by way of apology. 'What gives, Miss Digby?'

'Oh nothing of any magnitude. The mayor's office has telephoned twice so far, I have half the reporters on the West Coast squashed in your office—'

'In my office?' I butted in. 'What's wrong with your office?'

'I am in it, Mr. Preston,' she retorted calmly. 'I have work to do. Your room is empty. In addition to which, I felt you might prefer to have this conversation private at both ends. However, if you'll hang on I'll call them—'

'No, no,' I groaned. At my age I should have known better than to cross words with Digby the minute I got out of bed. 'You were quite right, of course. Since you don't regard either the mayor or the press as of any significance, why did you call?'

'That man has just been on the line. Mr. Lasky from Larchville. You said—'

I was awake finally.

'Yes, I remember. What's the story on Handford?'

Florence Digby hates to be interrupted. I could imagine her mouth set into the familiar prim lines as she replied.

'Nothing, Mr. Preston. Not an incriminating word.'

Sadly I said:

'That's a real disappointment. Could you just read out what you have, please?'

She read. It was a brief history, and couldn't have been more innocuous. Almost.

'What?' I shouted excitedly. 'Read that bit again.'

She read it again.

'And he guarantees this information?'

'Certainly. What is there to guarantee? There's nothing here you wouldn't want the people next door to know.'

'You're right,' I soothed.

And she was right. Nothing you wouldn't want the people next door to know. But the people in another town, another state. They might come into an entirely different category. I thanked her, told her to get rid of the newshounds, and I'd try to get into the office some time in the afternoon.

After that I rang the Handford

Construction Company. Paula Brickman tried to stall me off but I managed to convince her this wasn't the day for it. When I finally got through to the man he wasn't anxious to see me.

'I've got a very tight schedule here today, Preston,' he said brusquely. 'Let's make it some other time.'

'Today,' I replied flatly. 'To be exact, in an hour from now. You see me then, or I'm going to the Vale City *Clarion* with all I know about you and Jeannie Benson and Larchville.'

There was a gasp at the other end.

'This is blackmail,' he said steadily.

'So it is,' I agreed. 'One hour. Where'll I see you?'

He hesitated.

'At my house.'

He told me the address, and I said if he wasn't there at ten forty-five I'd head for the *Clarion* Office, then hung up.

Twenty minutes later I left the apartment. Since talking to Handford I was ahead one shower, one shave, two cups of coffee and two Old Favourites. I was fit to appear on the street again. Downstairs Frank, the day man, smiled widely when he saw me.

'Hi, Mr. Preston. Say, they gave you a good spread today, huh?'

He waved a copy of the *Bugle*. I muttered something civil.

'There were some newspaper guys here

216

early on,' he continued chattily. 'Said you weren't answering the telephone. I came up to see if you were O.K. and found you'd left it off the hook. You musta been pretty tired, I guess.'

I forced myself to remember the man meant well.

'I guess so. Thanks for re-connecting it, Frank.'

'Ah, that's O.K. You was out cold anyway, so I told the scribes you weren't in. Hope that was all right?'

He looked at me anxiously, and I was glad I'd held my tongue. The reporters would have made mincemeat of me if Frank had let them through.

'You did fine, Frank. I needed the sleep.'

Five minutes after that I was headed for the outskirts of Monkton City, nose pointed inland.

*   *   *

Walter F. Handford lived in a small but clearly expensive property in the desirable section of out-town Vale. It was ten-forty as I braked beside a line of well-cut shrubs which served as a partial screen for the house. I wondered what complications there would be inside by way of help. A man in Handford's position had no need of doing his own cooking and cleaning, so there was probably somebody else

217

in the house, maybe more than one.

I rang a mellow-toned bell, and almost immediately he opened the door himself. There was no smile this time, no cordiality.

'Come in.'

I stepped inside and followed him into a low, pleasant room which had two pairs of open french doors leading out into a small flagged terrace. Nobody asked me to sit down.

'What is it you want?' demanded Handford.

There was an old-style Colonial fireplace in the room, and although there wasn't any fire, Handford stationed himself in front of it. With his grim unfriendly expression he reminded me of one Barrett, of Wimpole Street fame. Only this wasn't a play.

'You told me a tale the other day,' I said gently. 'It wasn't all true. In fact, a good deal of it was plain lies.'

'Really?' he replied, without interest. 'I probably couldn't see any reason why I should discuss my personal affairs with anybody like you.'

'Don't be rude to me,' I begged. 'I'm sensitive. And you have a choice as of now. You can either discuss your personal affairs with somebody like me, or we can talk the whole thing over down at Vale Police Headquarters.'

'Talk what over?' he asked loftily. 'There isn't anything to talk about.'

I sighed, tapped an Old Favourite from the

218

pack and lit it.

'My call must have upset you. After what you read in the papers this morning, you probably imagined the whole thing was over. You could just put it out of your mind as a nasty little incident, and a year from now you'd have difficulty in remembering the details.'

A quick smirk flitted across his face.

'Papers? I don't quite understand.'

'Oh yes you do. I'll bet you've been reading every word that's been printed about the Ruby Capone murder, and everything that's happened since. With the pay-off story this morning the whole thing seems to be settled. No more threat of any inconvenience to Walter F. Handford.'

Handford inclined his head slightly.

'I know what you're talking about of course. Yes, I did see in the paper that you'd cleaned up some narcotics ring or something like that. Since I'd met you, I was naturally interested.'

'Naturally,' I returned drily. 'There was the fact you knew me, plus the fact that Ruby Capone was Jeannie Benson.'

He tried to look astonished, but he wasn't very good.

'J—Jeannie? Oh no, you must be mistaken about that. Why the Capone girl was nothing more than a cheap—'

'She was nothing more than you turned her into, liar,' I snapped.

His eyes became ice, and his fists clenched. I

wondered if he might take a swing at me.

'Did you say liar?'

'Yup. That's what you are, Handford. A big four-flushing liar. And if you're going to do anything with those fists, come on. I'd like an excuse to lam into you for Jeannie's sake.'

Instead of coming for me, he crumpled suddenly. All the confidence oozed out of him, and the lines of his face sank into despair. He sat down heavily.

'How did you know?'

'A man named Cyrus Lasky told me,' I informed him.

The puzzlement on his face was not assumed.

'Lasky? I don't know anybody by that name.'

'Maybe not. But he sure knows about you. Everything that ever happened back in Larchville. He's a P.I. over there.'

'P.I. ?'

'Like me,' I explained. 'Lasky put me onto you. He did more than that. Unless I'm mistaken it was the same man told Jeannie you were making a sucker out of her—'

'No—no. Not that. Please don't say that—' he pleaded.

'What else do you call it? You got another word for it, Handford? Here's a nice girl, I like the look of her. Like to get her in bed for a while, few months maybe. That would be something. But marriage? Uh, uh. That's out.

220

No marriage. Let's think up a dandy little story to cover that route. And what story did you come up with, huh? The one about your poor ailing wife in a mental hospital. Oh, it was a good one. Plenty of violins, and the bit at the end of the second movement was a lulu. The part where you jerk out the truth. She wouldn't be in there if it weren't for you, and your drunk driving. Brother, you really laid it on with a trowel. You've never been in an automobile accident in your life. Never been married either. Because that woman over there in the sanatorium, Mrs. Walter Handford, she isn't your wife, is she, Handford. She's your mother.'

I spat the last part out forcibly. Handford winced as he sat with his head buried in his hands.

'You're, you're making it sound all wrong,' he protested feebly.

'Wrong,' I replied scornfully. 'Oh sure it was wrong. But it isn't me making it sound that way. You did that, you made it wrong from the start. You took a decent kid like Jeannie Benson and turned her into Ruby Capone. You did that, Handford. There isn't a court in the state can touch you for that, but they can act quick enough on your next little trick, the one where you got too ambitious. And turned to murder.'

He dragged his head quickly up and I wasn't looking at any kind of mask any more. The stark horror coming from that troubled face belonged to Walter F. Handford.

'No,' he whispered hoarsely. 'No, you're wrong. I didn't kill her. Didn't kill Jeannie. You're making a terrible mistake.'

'I don't think so,' I went on relentlessly. 'Jeannie got fed up with things, didn't she? Wanted a home, maybe a family of her own, and she couldn't see you providing them, could she? Something made her wonder whether everything was the way it should be with you. Whether there was something else besides a mentally sick wife keeping you apart. She was at the end of the line when she got in touch with Lasky—'

'No, wait. Wait a minute.'

Handford held up a hand in protest. This was a beaten man. He was all through with the hearts and flowers bit. Anything he was going to say now, I wanted to hear.

'If this Lasky told you Jeannie had been checking up on me he's a liar. It would never have entered her head to do a thing like that.' His face twisted. 'It was her good friend I have to thank for that. Francie Andrews.'

And that was something I hadn't thought of.

'Francie? Why should she care enough?' I wondered.

'According to her, she thought of Jeannie as a sister. Anyway she thought Jeannie was wasting her life on me, so she set out to check up on my past.'

'And it was she who told Jeannie about your mother?'

He nodded.

'I imagine it must have been. I never had a chance to explain—'

'Explain what? Why you lied to her, seduced her, drove her nearly out of her mind?'

'Listen, you've got to believe me, somebody has to believe me. I had no way of knowing it was going to turn out like this.'

He was throwing himself on my mercy, but I didn't have any spare. I was thinking what happened to a nice girl who once trusted somebody else, leaned on him. She leaned on Handford, and she wound up dead. I stared at him without pity.

'Tell me the rest. Give me a reason I shouldn't take you down to headquarters and have you booked for murder. And get a grip on yourself. You make me sick.'

'All right.' He sat wringing his hands together, and trying to bring himself under control. 'I'll tell you. I didn't kill Jeannie, what do you take me for? But I'll tell you. You were quite right about—about mother. I've been using her as an excuse for not getting married. It always seemed like a good idea till now.'

He looked quickly at me to see whether I could understand what a good thing it was to have an ironclad excuse for avoiding marriage. I stared back stonily.

'Well, Francie found out and told her about

223

it. Jeannie didn't even bother to ask me whether it was true. She didn't even ask.'

He was complaining now.

'Why should she?' I demanded. 'You'd only have had to admit it was.'

Handford made no reply to that.

'Anyway she left town. I'd no idea where she went. Then about two months ago a man called me. Said he'd seen my lady friend and wanted to talk to me about it. I met him in a bar and he started talking about this Capone woman and how bad it would be if an important man like me were to get linked with her in the newspapers. I thought he was crazy, told him I never heard of anybody named Capone. Then he produced a photograph and I saw it was Jeannie he was talking about. I asked him where she was, and when he told me I didn't believe him. He told me to come and see for myself. So I did, I met him the same night and we drove to Monkton City and I saw her. Saw what she'd turned into. Listen, I'm not looking for any sympathy from you, but if you'd seen the difference, seen what had become of Jeannie Benson in just a few months, you'd have realised better how I felt. Well, that was the way she'd elected to go. I still had my position in this community to think about.'

'So when the man suggested it ought to be worth a few dollars for him to keep his mouth shut, you paid?' I demanded.

'Yes. In some other business I'd have told him to go to hell, but in mine, no. Most of my stuff relies on civic contracts, hospitals, drainage and so on. Taxpayers can get awfully righteous about who they spend their money with.'

I interrupted sharply.

'It's breaking my heart having to listen to how vulnerable you are, a big important man like you. The point is, you paid. How much?'

'Not a great deal. This man seemed to have assessed fairly well how much it would be worth to me. He just used to take a hundred or so every other week. No really big sums.'

'This man, did he have a name?'

'If he had, he never told it to me. Just said I could call him Took.'

Took. Of course, it had to be Took. That was why Rose had the picture and the telephone number. If ever she got in really bad trouble, the man at the other end, Handford, would have to get her out. She would have known Took was putting the black on somebody. Known that it was something to do with Ruby Capone, even though she may not have known all the details. I doubted whether Took had in fact ever trusted her with any of it. She'd probably watched him use the telephone at some time and worked the rest out for herself.

'I know the guy,' I informed him. 'He's had to leave town for his health. So he was blackmailing you, but not too hard. What happened then?'

'Nothing. Naturally, I didn't let Jeannie know I'd found out where she was—'

'Naturally? Why naturally? Did it occur to you that you could save that girl? You could have taken her out of that dump and brought her back here and married her. Did you think of that?'

He flushed and kept silent for a while.

'All right,' I said disgustedly. 'Get on with the memoirs.'

'Well, things continued as before. This man Took would telephone me and suggest a loan, and I would send him money. Then, the other night, Jeannie came. Came here to the house.'

'Did you expect her?'

'No. In fact I was about to leave for a meeting when she arrived. She—she'd changed.'

'Surprise, surprise,' I sneered.

Handford disregarded that.

'She was coarse and cheap-looking. She had dyed her hair and her clothes were awful. On top of that she was drunk. She came in and began to make a scene. Somehow she'd found out about the money I was paying Took. She said some terrible things about me—oh, don't look like that, I know I deserved them. Most of them anyway. I always keep a few drinks here, and she knew where to find them. She was drinking straight scotch, and right from the bottle. I asked her why she'd come back and she told me in no uncertain terms. Her life had been ruined by two men, she said. The first was her father. According to what she said, her father was a famous gangster, though I didn't actually believe that. Jeannie told me she hadn't found out about him until a couple of years ago. When she did she walked out, and hadn't seen him since.' Handford looked up at me. 'I never heard of any racketeer named Benson, did you? Think she was telling the truth?'

'Quien sabe?' I shrugged. 'Tell me what else she said.'

'You don't have to be told who the other man was. It was me.' He shivered slightly. 'I'm not going into the details of what she said about me. But that night was what she'd been planning for. That night she was going to get even with us both. I asked her what she meant by that, and then she told me an extraordinary tale.'

He looked up again as if doubtful that I'd believe him.

'Go ahead. What tale?'

'Jeannie said she'd done what she did, taken a job at this so-called club for the sole reason that she wanted to break her father. Wanted to get a lot of evidence about his activities so she could turn it over to the police. You think that could be true?'

I ignored the question.

'And how was she going to get back at you?'

By way of answer Handford got up and went to a cupboard. The bottle rattled noisily against the glass as he poured himself a stiff measure of brandy. Then he tossed it down in a way that showed little awareness of the label. He sighed then and turned back to me.

'As I've told you, the girl was high. Her plan for me was simple. She was going to shoot herself full of dope right here in the house. I have a woman who helps around the house, usually gets here just before eight in the morning. Jeannie said quite calmly that she would still be unconscious then, and the woman would find her. "Dope-girl found in Councilman's Bed" was the headline she taunted me with.'

'You could have explained it away,' I suggested. 'Better still, the moment she tried it you could've called the police yourself.'

'No, she'd thought of that. I had a choice, she told me. If I let her do it her way, she might choose to keep quiet about my mother not being my wife. It's possibly hard for you to understand, but if that comes out, I shall be forced to sell up here in Vale, and move on. Anyhow, I argued and argued with her but it wasn't any use. She was determined to do it, drunk or not. She—she took out this hypodermic—'

He rubbed a hand over his face where the sweat was starting to roll down his cheeks.

'I tried to take it from her, but she was like a wild creature. Finally she stuck the needle in her leg, and pushed the plunger. She was laughing, Preston, that was what made it so horrible. She was laughing.'

'Then what happened.'

'Nothing, for a while. She seemed to sober up a little at first. Then she began to gasp for breath. She staggered around the room, trying to get to the window. It was awful to hear her fighting to breathe like that. I couldn't do anything to help. Suddenly she just fell down over there.'

He pointed to a spot by the wall.

'I tried to rouse her but it wasn't any use. And then, after several minutes, I realised she was dead. It seemed incredible, or maybe I just didn't want to believe it. But Jeannie was dead.'

'Of course she was,' I snapped. 'Pumping a narcotic into your body while there's alcohol there is almost certain death. Especially the quantity she used. What did you do next?'

'I sat down for a while, and thought. I knew that whatever I did mustn't be done in panic. I couldn't let her be found where she was, so that meant moving the body. At the same time I also couldn't fail to put in an appearance at the meeting. There were a couple of items up for discussion which I was closely concerned with, and I would have had no reason to offer for not showing. Then I remembered Took.

229

He was already the only person who knew of any connection between Jeannie and me. From what I'd seen of him, he wasn't the type of man to be squeamish about the job. I called him, told him I wanted something done. I offered a thousand dollars since I was fairly sure that would bring him here fast. He came all right. When he saw Jeannie he immediately made the fee twice what I'd mentioned. I agreed of course. Then he made another condition. In case he was caught with the body on the highway he wanted to be certain I didn't just deny the whole thing. He wanted my car. So I let him have that, too. Then he made me help him carry her out of the house. We took her between us, as though she were drunk or ill. We put her in the front, next to Took and he drove her away. That was the last time I saw her.'

And then went to the meeting and reported the car stolen when he left it. That was pretty cool thinking, I reflected. Cool. Or cold-blooded.

Handford went to get himself another drink. I thought about what he'd told me. It all fitted in well enough. I doubted whether the girl had intended to kill herself. She wouldn't know that heroin and whisky don't go together. Took would have dumped her in her apartment, then gone back to the Peek-a-Boo until the place closed. It seemed a probability, though I'd never know for certain, that Took had tipped off Vander about her death. He probably wouldn't have mentioned Handford's part in it. Simply told the boss that he'd found the girl dead in her apartment and thought Vander would want to know. And he'd want to know all right, because he'd been wondering just what to do about Jeannie himself, or Ruby as he knew her. Whether Took was acting on Vander's instructions or not when he discovered the body a few hours later was again a matter for surmise. The death had pointed the way for the elimination of the real threat, which was Lola Wade. After that one broke, the police were already looking for Benito, and he'd turned up in Monkton City with two of his goons. It was obvious that Benito would be trying to find out just how much the police had on him, and try to block up as many channels as he could before the law could find him. I hadn't forgotten that when I put Rose Schwartz on the local to L.A. it was Benito's strong-arm squad who were waiting outside the station for me. They wouldn't know what my connection was with the boss. What they would have seen was a nosy private investigator helping one of Vander's girls to leave town, at a time when leaving town was a bad thing to be doing. They would have told Vander to get something done about it, and Jammy or somebody like him would have climbed on to the train and forced Rose off. Vander, too, would only know me as a man who was showing an unhealthy interest in Ruby Capone. If Rose was going to be eliminated it would be a sound move to do it in my apartment, thus incriminating me in the eyes of the law and warning me to lay off all at the same time.

While I was busy with these thoughts, I was forgetting about Handford. When I looked across at him he was contemplating an empty glass again.

'Well?' he demanded.

'Well what?'

'What are you going to do about it, about me?'

'I don't know,' I told him frankly. 'I'll have to think about it.'

'Well, I know,' said a new voice. 'And I don't have to think about it.'

Handford and I swung round at the same moment. From behind the floor-length curtaining beside an open french door walked a man with a blue automatic in his fist. He was Rudy Benito. The suave, highly-polished character I was used to was gone. He looked rumpled now, in need of a shave. His eyes were slightly bloodshot, and his shirt was soiled. The suit looked as if it had been slept in. All the years of acquisition had fallen away from him overnight and Benito was right back where he started. A gutter-rat behind a gun.

'What's this about,' demanded Handford. 'Who are you?'

To do the man justice, he didn't sound in the least afraid of the gun. And it was pointed at him not me.

'Me?' hissed Benito. 'I'm her father, that's who.'

Handford blanched now, and seemed to realise he was looking at death.

'This is all wrong, Benito—' I began

'Shut up,' he snapped. 'I'm going to kill this guy. I don't have anything against you, Preston, but if you get in my way, you'll get some of this too.'

'K—kill me?'

There was disbelief in Handford's voice but not on his face. I was trying to work out some way in which to distract Benito's attention long enough to get out the .38. But he'd been in too many spots like this. He'd stationed himself at an angle where he could watch both of us easily.

'My little Gina,' he whispered. 'She kep' on changing her name. She figured she din' have no chance as Gina Benito, an' I can see where she was prob'y right. The name she wound up wit', Ruby Capone, that Ruby never had a chance either. Anybody coulda tol' ya what would happen wid a dame like dat. But Jeannie Benson, she was O.K. Jeannie, she was up dere on cloud seven, and she hadda good chance. Jeannie coulda made it fine, 'cept for you. You're a pig.'

'Now, wait a minute—' shouted Handford.

'What for?' snarled Benito.

233

The automatic cracked sharply, once, twice. Handford clutched at his middle, shocked surprise large on his face. A thin rivulet of blood ran between his fingers. Benito walked across and spat in his face.

'This ain't for Ruby Capone, pal. Nobody cares what happen to a dame like dat. This is for Jeannie.'

Holding the gun close against Handford's chest he squeezed the trigger again, and the smell of cordite was sharp in the room. Handford screamed and fell backwards, his head striking with a sickening thud against the corner of a table as he went.

There was nothing I could do to stop Benito. He was still half-faced to me, the muscles in his neck jumping with the emotion which didn't show on his face.

With a last look at the bloody mess at his feet he turned to me.

'That was smart of ya, Preston. I wasn' kiddin' back dere. I'da blasted ya sure, ya got in my way.'

His tone was almost conversational. I wasn't feeling so calm. My mouth was so dry I had to cough before I could speak.

'My turn now?'

His eyes became wide with surprise.

'Whaffor? You done alright by me. In my book you're O.K. Him, the pig, it was him I wanted.'

'How did you get on to him?' I queried.

Benito chuckled. It was impossible to realise he'd just stamped out a human life.

'I din'. You came here, I follow. After wha' happen last night, I got to wonderin'. 'Bout you mostly. You're pretty smart feller. I din' believe all dat crap on da radio, in da papers. I figure to myself, dat Preston. He'sa know someting dan we hear so far. Someting maybe even he don' tell da cops. Maybe I watch Preston a lil bit. I learn someting. You come outta your place dis mornin', I follow ya. You bring me here, and den I remember 'bout dis pig and my Gina. You're pretty smart feller, Preston. Keep da change outta da five Gs.'

He was still holding the gun loosely in his hand. I couldn't be sure of what he intended to do.

'What happens now?' I asked him. 'Somebody could have heard those shots.'

He shrugged.

'Maybe. Who cares? I'm all t'rough. Washed up.'

He said it without any inflection of regret or self-pity. I said:

'Not necessarily. You could be over the hills and far away before the law gets here. Not much I could do to stop you as long as you're holding the gun.'

'Ah, whassa use? Wha' for? The cops— You tink I worry 'bout dose guys? I bin arrested before. More times'n you got fingers an' toes. I tell ya, Preston, if the blue boys was my only trouble, I wouldn't have no troubles.'

'All right, then why do you say you're finished?' I asked.

'Because da word is out, peeper. Da word is out. Kinda funny really. I sent out da word on so many guys in my time, I never figure one day maybe it's gonna be me.'

He smiled briefly. What he was telling me was that the mob were looking for him. They had decided the operation was in danger because of Benito, and so he had to go. It was a very unusual thing for the word to go out on a wheel of Benito's standing.

'Why are they doing it?' I wanted to know.

'Ya know da rules? Once ya can't trust somebody no more, he's gotta be rubbed out, ya know? That's me, Benito. Day don't trust me no more. Some of dis stuff my Gina give da cops, it's very confidential stuff. On'y a few guys could possibly know some of it. I'm one of dose guys, the others got clean noses, it leaves me. Right?'

'Yes,' I protested, 'but they can't think you'd provide information against yourself.'

'Sure they don't. But they think I'm starting to talk too much, talk to da wrong people. Gettin' careless. And a guy who will talk so careless he gives information that can put him away, what will such a guy say about other people? A guy like dat is a bad risk. I could tell about Gina, explain to them dat way, but I ain't goin' to. Dat's family business. I'm fifty

236

years old, Preston. In my business, dat's some kinda record. Dead years ago I shoulda bin. I'm lucky I should live so long. So now it's finished O.K. Wid Gina gone, I'm not complainin'. Ya gotta rod?'

I nodded.

'A .38.'

'Give it to me.'

Very carefully I took out the weapon and handed it over. He watched closely, which was one of the reasons he'd got to be fifty years old. When the gun was in his spare hand he grunted with satisfaction and slipped it into his pocket.

There was a thunderous knocking at the door.

'Open up here. This is the police.'

Benito grinned crookedly.

'You seem like a reglar guy, Preston. Do something for a customer, huh?'

'Like what?'

'Like put some flowers on my Gina sometimes, huh? Here.'

He took out his wallet and tossed it to me. 'Dere's four-five hundred bucks in dere. I won't need it where I'm going. Make 'em all choice blooms, huh?'

I nodded, and put the wallet away. There was more noise outside now as the police started kicking at the street door.

'Get outta here, ya lousy cops,' shouted Benito.

237

Running to the hall he snapped a quick shot at the door. The banging stopped immediately. There was a sound of running feet.

'Dat's right, ya lousy bulls. This is Benito, Rudy Benito. Ya better run.'

He screamed like an insane man and fired another wasted slug into the heavy panels of the door. From outside a voice shouted:

'Benito, throw out your gun and come out with your hands up.'

By way of answer he threw a vase through the window beside the door. Glass was still tinkling to the ground as he fired again.

'I'm comin' out all right,' he shouted through the empty frame. 'Ya better hide if ya don' wanna get killed.'

Then he took the .38 from his pocket and slipped the safety catch. Standing to one side he opened the street door.

'Here I come.'

He rushed suddenly into the opening, squeezing both triggers as fast as he could. There were other shots and he stopped half way to the street, one gun dropping from useless fingers. With an effort he brought up his good hand and fired again. Once. This time there were three shots in rapid succession, each ploughing into his tottering frame and punching him first one way, then another. He pitched heavily forward on his face.

I went back into the room and went to where Handford lay. Kneeling down beside him, I was holding his wrist, looking for a pulse beat when they came in. Four grim-faced patrol officers with guns in their hands stormed suddenly into the room.

'Up,' snapped one.

I got up.

A second man went to Handford.

'This guy is cold,' he announced.

Another was patting me all over, looking for a weapon.

'Clean,' he muttered.

'Who are you?'

I told them who I was.

'And him?'

I told them about Handford.

'The other man, the hoodlum. Said he was Rudy Benito. That right?'

'I wouldn't know. That's who he said he was, but I've never seen him before,' I replied.

'Hah,' snorted one. 'That was never Benito. Benito, he knew about guns. That guy out there just now, he couldn't hit a barn door at ten feet. Lucky for us.'

Luckier than you know, officer, luckier than you know.

CHAPTER FIFTEEN

A week later I called at a house with a porch painted bright green. She must have seen me coming up the path because she opened the door almost at once. She smiled uncertainly.

'Hallo, Francie. Could I come in?'

'Of course.'

We went into the same room, the one where the eavesdropping Hec would be unsuccessful. We even sat in the same seats.

'I've been reading a lot about you in the papers,' she said tentatively. 'Guess you've been too busy to get very far looking for Jeannie.'

'No,' I contradicted. 'It all tied together. As far as I can find out, Francie, you're the only real friend Jeannie Benson ever had.'

'Had? You mean, something's happened to her?'

Her lip trembled, and I thought she might be going to cry.

'I think we're going to have to assume that,' I said gently. 'None of the usual agencies has been able to turn anything up. I'm sorry to tell you like this, but I think we must assume death.'

She did cry then, a few large tears rolling slowly down her cheeks.

'I'm sorry, Mr. Preston, didn't mean to cry. Guess I sort of expected something of the kind. Maybe it's as well she didn't live to find out how rotten her friend Walter Handford was. I never had a high opinion of him, as you know, but even I never dreamed he was mixed up with people like that awful gangster man,

240

Benito. That was a piece of bad luck for you being there with Handford when that hoodlum came. Was it really true what they said in the papers about Handford having some link with that terrible club in Monkton City?'

'True,' I confirmed. 'Handford was certainly tied in with the Peek-a-Boo Club in some way. Matter of fact, it's about Handford I came to see you. It doesn't matter any more really, it's just my curiosity. But you knew Handford's so-called wife was really his mother. You told Jeannie about it. So why couldn't you tell me when I called here before?'

She made a face.

'Yes, I'm sorry about that. I wondered later whether I should have told you. But Jeannie made me swear never to tell a soul. Said she wanted to be the only one who knew. She was talking, you know, wild talk about revenge and so forth. She said she wanted that secret kept until it was time for her to expose it. As I say, she was just talking, but a promise is a promise. She'll never get that revenge now, will she?'

'I guess not.'

A few minutes later she walked with me to the door. The sea-shell path shone whitely in the sun. I held out my hand.

'Well, goodbye, Francie, and thanks.'

'Goodbye. Shall I be seeing you again, maybe. One day?'

I turned and looked at her. She was very

241

striking as she stood in the green frame.

'Maybe, some day.'

It's a throw of the dice. If you're lucky you're Francie Andrews. If not, you could be Gina Benito. I shivered as a low grey cloud obscured the sun. Later it would rain.

We hope you have enjoyed this Large Print book. Other Chivers Press or G.K. Hall & Co. Large Print books are available at your library or directly from the publishers.

For more information about current and forthcoming titles, please call or write, without obligation, to:

Chivers Press Limited
Windsor Bridge Road
Bath BA2 3AX
England
Tel. (01225) 335336

OR

G.K. Hall & Co.
P.O. Box 159
Thorndike, Maine 04986
USA
Tel. (800) 223-2336

All our Large Print titles are designed for easy reading, and all our books are made to last.